T0077926

# THE PATSY

## BEING TAKEN FOR A RUN

CORY PERALA

authorHOUSE®

AuthorHouse™
1663 Liberty Drive
Bloomington, IN 47403
www.authorhouse.com
Phone: 833-262-8899

Published by AuthorHouse 07/20/2020

ISBN: 978-1-7283-6718-7 (sc)
ISBN: 978-1-7283-6717-0 (e)

Library of Congress Control Number: 2020913151

Print information available on the last page.

# CONTENTS

# A PORTRAIT

"Here, I would like you to draw my portrait Ernest," says James handing out cash.

"I would be happy to do that for you, is there anything you'll be looking for in the portrait?" says Ernest with his tiny black sun glasses resting on his nose. His black curly hair and short pudgy body type speaks for his large ego without saying a word.

"All I'm looking for is what you see Ernest, you're the painter," says James.

"I'd like this much more if you give me something to go by."

Ernest the painter and James the portrait client sit inside a coffee shop with the loud espresso machine running in the back with a busy line of a dozen people waiting to get the best cup of coffee in town. Amazingly, one person is able to run the coffee shop by themselves. Turning out a hot beverage in thirty seconds is a great talent for the highly motivated entrepreneur.

"I am giving you something to go by, I'm looking for what you see," says James with a full grown beard and tall lanky body. His blue eyes and the wrinkles around them express his old age that much more. He is roughly fifty years old, twenty-five years past his prime.

"I understand."

"So, just by looking at me right now what do you see?"

"I see a gentleman who has just ended a lifelong venture. What it was? I do not know, but either it ended really great or very sour," says Ernest.

"Now that you see that, what do you see other than what it actually is?"

"Ah…..wow, that is hard to do."

"You're right, it is hard to do. There can be a different definition of sourness and greatness, success and failure, opportunity and setback."

"Perception makes up ninety percent of our world. You just can't change that and alter our reality. Logic and reason will always be working against you."

"Your right logic and reason will always work against me, so I will always be working against it. You see, in order to make the impossible possible, logic and reason is the barrier of impossible. We must open our minds and do crazy shit to make the impossible happen."

"Well, I've got to get going, do you have a time available to do the portrait. Plan for about six hours," says Ernest.

"I've got six hours tomorrow at noon, how bout that?"

"Tomorrow at noon works great, my talent and creativity peaks at about four in the afternoon. This is great timing to put the finishing touches on the portrait."

Ernest alternates from looking through his sun glasses resting on his nose to tilting his head down making eye contact with James. Making eye contact confirms the appointment for tomorrow.

"I'll see you tomorrow," says James getting out of his chair to walk out of the coffee shop. There is a buckle in his old knee having little cartilage, just bone grinding on bone.

Walking kitty corner across the traffic jam in the street, the rush hour commute has come to a stand still at this early hour of seven in the morning. Upon getting across the street, James goes into a thrift store.

Walking up to the front counter where a tall lady is working on keeping the books for yesterday's transactions, James notices the brunette recognize him. She smiles and begins to open her mouth to say something before James starts the conversation.

"How are you Gwen?" says James.

"I was doing swell, then I came into work doing alright, and then I see you and now everything is fine," says Gwen with a hysterical look on her face.

"That's good."

"Do you have a woman of your own yet?"

"I haven't found a woman to put up with my shit. My shit stinks, it stinks very bad. My shit stinks so much; I don't even wipe my ass anymore."

"Oh, that's more than a problem, that's a problem and a half."

"I just haven't found a woman to wipe my ass yet."

"Good luck with that."

"It's a hidden gem, a diamond to be exact. What do you think? Is this too good to be true?"

"Ah….obviously yeah, love isn't perfect you know."

"Well, James Bond and Batman all lived without a woman in their life."

"Those aren't real people James. They had women come and go briefly in their life."

"Don't give me that Santa Claus bull shit Gwen. I believe what I want to believe."

"Sooner or later you will have to face reality," says Gwen with a smile on her face looking down at the financial statements.

"That works both ways you know. Rainbows and Unicorns aren't the most realistic and practical fantasy either."

✑

The next day at noon, James walks through the doors of Ernest's studio at the top floor of his Baltimore apartment. James wears a black long sleeve dress shirt, red tie, and black dress pants. The studio room has one wall perpendicular to the windows looking outside with nothing on them, this is the wall Ernest will face to paint James's portrait. The living room furniture, dining table, stove, and fridge is on the opposite side of the studio where Ernest and James are working. A room next to the door entrance has a shower and toilet. Ernest is working on his color palette and takes a chair from the dinning table for James to sit on while he creates the portrait.

"I can't wait to get started. After painting, when will it be ready?" says James tightening the red tie around his neck.

"We need a good day for it to dry and set in. Oh, and good news, I had a dream last night that I was painting inside the Sistine Chapel with Michelangelo himself," says Ernest.

"Are you afraid of heights?"

Yeah well, I was not hanging upside down swinging in mid-air by a two by four attached to a harness in my dream painting with Michelangelo. Then it would have been a nightmare. No, I was on the ground painting on canvas and preparing color palettes."

"Sounds great let's get started."

As James sits down he immediately puts on a big smile to widen his long bearded face. His long hair and lanky body make him look skinny. As sunlight shines through, one side of James's face is darker than the other, which is Ernest's intention for the painting. For the first thirty minutes, Ernest sizes up James's facial features to visualize the design of the face.

The long and arduous process of the face takes four hours with another ninety minutes for the background and body from the shoulders up to be completed. The last brush stroke is Ernest's signature written with a big "E" and smaller sized letters for the rest of the name.

"There, all done," says Ernest resting the palete down on his chair.

"May I see," says James.

"Yeah, take a look."

James takes his first glance saying, "Wow wonderful!"

The portrait is an identical match to James with a gradual darkening grade from right to left.

"This is like reading a book about my life at the present time. My focused eyes show I'm serious about life, the wide smile shows my craving for excitement and enthusiasm, and the broad cheeks and chin represent nothing stopping me."

The background of the painting changes from gold to brown, light gold on the right and ascending to dark brown colors on the left. James is slightly rotated towards the windows where the light comes from. His Adam's apple protrudes on top of the dress shirt collar and below the chin. His brown hair is not evenly parted, but is resting more on the portrait's right towards the light. His blue eyes inject cold admiration into the perception of the viewer. The blue eyes stick out so much due to being the only shade of blue on the portrait.

# DYNAMIC LENDERS

## Twenty-Five Years Earlier

"I'm obsessed with the free markets; consumers looking for the most value for their money and businesses looking for the highest profit. They contradict each other, but together they achieve a balance," says James

"How do you grow a profit?" asks Griffin.

The amazing thing is profit is made by focusing on people, not money. Yes, you need money to get profit, but you need people to get money. I'm a bit of a business man myself, as a grad from Wharton's Business School, I aspire to be in angel investing. I love it; in fact, I can't get enough of it. I watch company quarterly financial statements all day. Finding the next hidden gem will make or break a person."

Griffin and James are seated in a blue 1995 Buick Regal, driving down Interstate 95 in Baltimore. Griffin is driving with a cigarette in his mouth, holding onto the cigarette with his forefinger and thumb. The two look through the front windshield as if watching TV show reels of the future rather than focusing all their attention on the road. James has a dumb founded look knowing the game Griffin is playing with asking questions to lay out what the future may look like even if the answers to some of his questions are impractical and not a reality.

"I can relate with the next Microsoft dorm room entity. What's the key to finding the next hidden gem?"

"The key? The key is all about where the creator's motivation comes from, which can be answered by asking two questions."

"What questions are they?"

"What made you decide to go into business for yourself? Then I will ask, where did you get the idea? The first question seeks motivation, what does the second question seek?"

"The second question determines when, where, and whom the originality of the idea came from. The best business ideas come from a random child mindset. A sense of play as if it were. If I see that and like the idea, BOOM, I'm in, all in as a matter of fact," says Griffin smacking the top of the steering wheel with the palm of his hand to emphasize the Boom with enthusiasm. James changes to a more comfortable position in the passenger seat, resting his right elbow on the window frame and hand on his temple in deep thought. Upon realizing the thought that crosses his mind, he points to the front windshield to begin describing his idea.

"Interesting, that reminds me of a story, let me tell it to you," says James.

"I'm all ear," says Griffin.

"There was this family homestead out in the woods three miles from a small rural town. The family worked, both father and mother at the pickle factory with three kids. The kids grew up dirt poor, with nothing but clothes and food. One child was interested in science, one in reading and writing, and one was socially interested in people. The amazing thing is they all moved to a nearby city and produced massive amounts of work with their skills and ability," says James.

"Their work was produced within and created with tools, but the work of the great is not produced over night. Nope, this requires hours of practice," says Griffin trying to build onto and explain James's story in more detail.

"There's more to tell," James is not happy from being interrupted.

"What's that?" says Griffin who is obviously enjoying the competition of adding to the same story, even though James was the first to tell the story.

"They were all successful in maintaining their lifestyle to produce the work they did."

"There is more to this, come on James, definitely more. We can talk about this scenario of internal motivation all day."

"Okay, what's the link between internal motivation and a single purpose focused on with all a person's attention? To take one hell of a risk and go all in, throwing all resources at the objective, thinking big, and putting oneself in circumstances where there is no return."

"I think the individual in this scenario will burn out quickly and lose sight of the objective. Breaks are needed, if the individual hits it too hard burn out could happen. They may give up entirely and all the money, time, and effort will be in vain."

"That is beyond the control of said individual, my analysis says, the individual will realize they can continue their effort upon realizing what they can and cannot control. Let's say the individual tries something different, does that not mean the purpose is still alive and just the strategy to get there has changed. Why repeat the same strategy if it does not work?"

"Very good observation, saying a strategy doesn't work does not change the end goal in mind. Rather than saying the goal is achieved directly, could the goal be achieved indirectly?"

"You mean accomplishing the goal by accident. Yes, this may happen, but with lower probability compared to directly going after a goal. I can relate indirectly accomplishing a goal by accident with my personal motto: It takes a village to raise a child."

"Precisely, let's go to the park for a game of chess, what do you say?" says James.

"Sure, only if I get the white pieces, the white pieces go first you know," says Griffin taking the exit off the interstate.

꙳

At the park, picnic tables are next to the green trees and festering ivy plants with thorns crawl up the base pillars of the shelter walls. Falling acorns from the trees above are hitting the tin on the roof of the shelter every so often. A swift breeze from the cool north air makes its way across the river to the hilly river bank in the park. As James and Griffin collaborate their mindful chess strategies, each holds their index finger on a temple deep in thought to get a better look at their visualizations.

As each player is thinking two moves ahead, the game shows itself to be of anticipation, strategy, the very characteristic they are focused on as being entrepreneurs. The hypothetical thinking that occurs from playing a game of what if I do this, then this happens. Cause and effect, pros and cons, strengths and weaknesses, aces in the hole and wild cards, this is what each player faces.

"I believe white pieces go first James," says Griffin.

"Oh, that's right," says James with a look of disbelief on his face.

"I can't wait to have my bishop end this game in check mate," says Griffin being confident and basically calling the move he will make to end the game. Being tooled with preparation, he knows a quick win with his bishop is the best way to defeat James's method of winning by attrition.

A young girl skips by while flaying her arms to the point of almost knocking the chess board off of the table. She continues skipping towards the swing set where all the other kids are playing. James loses his concentration on the game and squints his eyes in anger after losing sight of his futuristic check mate attempt.

James holds his breath to try and not burst out at the girl. His face is red with a white forehead and red cheeks having a clear imbalance and lack of homeostasis occur. Griffin is the opposite, with a smile on his face and looking at James's dismay, he likes the chaos and starts to move quickly each time it is his turn. By allowing

James less time to think about his checkmate, he tries to get out of the snare.

"Whew, that was close, I hope to get a new chess board in the event it breaks, it's made of marble you know?" says Griffin.

"I have changed my scheme to take out both of your bishops just to prove you wrong," says James.

"I create much anticipation to the fact that neither of my bishops will get taken out."

Griffin surprisingly moves his bishops in his first sequence of moves. The main pattern he uses is a zigzag. His bishops buy time and wait for James to deal with the pawns and knights. As Griffin moves his queen ahead two spaces. James mobilizes his strategy of attrition with flanking his bishop, knight, and rook to one side. Griffin castles his king to same side as James's flank. However, Griffin gets his bishop in between James's king and the flank to make a check. James moves forward, which allows the castling rooks to capture the James flank one by one. With Griffin's two bishops and a knight working on James's king, the end is in sight and the flank fails by James.

The game ends in exactly the same way Griffin predicted. The smirk on his face is that of a trickster. James almost throws a fit in disbelief, throwing his champion fists overhead with control. Even though there is no crowd to cheer him, he takes in the glory of victory.

"This is a flaw, next time I get to go first," says James.

"There are too many disadvantages to going second. I will not be able to have both bishops together on the board at the same time. I told you I was going to win with my bishops. Why didn't you try to focus more on capturing them?"

"I thought you were bluffing with a counter maneuver, which is why I flanked you."

"Nope, my counter maneuver, if there was one, was to defend my king with the rooks. Remember, you can castle by moving two pieces in one turn. I was two moves ahead of you after that point. Talk about an advantage."

"Play again? Best of three!" says James.

"No, I have work to do, maybe next time."

Griffin gets up to leave and has many acorns and pebbles of rock crunch under his feet with the steps he takes back to his Buick. His big frame makes his cap and glasses fit snug to his body. The sun is high in the sky at mid-day afternoon with many birds at the river banks. The river's cross bridge is a mile downstream, too far to see the busy crossing traffic.

⁂

Griffin and James wait in the cross walk of the intersection to have more of a shot at getting across. The traffic is busy on Broadway with traffic moving every which way. The difference between the social status of people is vast. A homeless man sits on the sidewalk next to the courthouse building. His hat with holes is on the sidewalk in front of him to collect money, but there is a nickel and a penny there. More than likely the nickel and penny is his, which is all that's left from the last purchase. The money does not pile up for long as he is sure to pocket it to be sure not to lose anything. The business professionals and their associates walk by on their phones, occupied in their business.

James brushes shoulders with a women walking in the oncoming direction.

"Oh, sorry about that. I did not see you there," says James.

"Look out where you're going would you!" says the woman wearing a black business suit with angry squinting eyes. Immediately, the woman turns around and raises a middle finger overhead and faces it behind her towards James.

"Let's go James, we're going to miss the subway train," says Griffin.

"Yep, we may need to get a taxi to arrive at the Don's Coffee shop in time," says James.

The two come to the stairs going to the subway tunnel and look at the subway schedule board of departure and arrival times.

"Hey, James do you see that?"

"See what? Where?"

"Up there across the street in the old apartment building, three floors from the top. Something is flashing, a light or a reflection perhaps."

The light was in an odd place as if someone was shining a spotlight out of their apartment window. The street and sidewalks were busy with a lot of people trying to get to their destination. Not a single person was walking slow or casually, not even the people walking and texting.

"Yes, I see it too. Looks to be more of a light to me, it's just probably a studio for photography."

"Taxi, taxi!" Griffin waves a taxi down on the curb of the street by running to catch up to it.

"Great job Griffin, you do have enough money for this cab right?"

"Me, you're the one with the money."

"You make two hundred grand a year and you can't cover a cab for fifteen miles."

"It's not how much money you make, it's how much money you keep that matters."

"Man, you're cheap," says Griffin shaking his head and looking in his wallet to see how much money he has.

&#x261E;

The cab pulls up to Don's Coffee Shop and the place is lit like a Christmas tree with every light on. The green lighted sign above flashes and is displayed in bold upper case letters. Rain just started and is becoming more and more steady.

"Will she commit?"

"There is no reason why she shouldn't, we are bonafide. Our business plan is great from a benefit/ cost ratio."

"I agree with that, but is she the type of person willing to give money to help others, to take money to prevent a loss. Oh, and on top of that invest money in a plan to take money? I'm not an accredited investor."

Griffin and James get out of the cab and pay the cab driver while leaving the door open of the back passenger door. Handing the driver the cash, the two then high step with high knees to avoid stepping in puddles of water, the ground is gravel with potholes. Inside, three

18

men sit at a corner booth talking silently and whispering to each other. The lights are dimly lit with low volume music playing over the speakers to give a calming and relaxing atmosphere. James immediately recognizes a woman seated in a booth nearest to the door and makes eye contact with her serious gaze. She doesn't blink and moves her eyes to look at the seat ahead of her and back to James.

"There she is, that's her," says James to Griffin patting his drenched hair and wiping his hand dry on his shirt.

James sits next to Griffin in the seat across from the lady in her fifties with a black and white top hat, black coat and white undershirt. Her hair is red with blue eyes. At first, she stairs down at her cup of espresso, stirring it with a spoon. Later, she stares at Griffin and switches from looking at his face to the window looking out towards the street. Thirty seconds go by with this going on. The pause is excruciatingly uncomfortable, a meeting without an initial greeting. The unwritten rules are the first person to break the silence is the first to blink.

"Well, let's start shall we. My name is Sharon, what are your names?"

"I'm Griffin and this is James," thinking it's appropriate to make the introduction due to Sharon's constant stare at him.

"Please explain your business for me."

"Yes, the business is a loan business to help people obtain money with bad credit. People with poor credit scores will get loans from us and be able to pay their bills. Loan terms will be one to five years with half the credit line going to the person taking out the loan and half staying with us. Any missed payments will be taken from the half that is with us to stay in good standing."

"You're saying the customer will be taking out a credit line for twice as much as they get," says Sharon.

"Yes, there is no interest on the payments and the business will keep 15% of the half they take as operating revenue. The initial setup fee is fifty dollars and with a target goal of three hundred members in the first year that is fifteen grand the first year," says James.

"When half of the loan is paid back, the remainder that is with us in reserve will be charged another 15% leaving 20% remaining to go to the borrower," says Griffin.

"Interesting, your cash flows will unlikely be steady if you charge one time fees, which will require wise money management."

Sharon is a loan shark with considerable experience. She needs to see the whites in her clients' eyes in order to make a deal with her serious money. She can tell James has the intellect and Griffin has the charismatic social skills. What she can't tell is their ability to stick to the business through thick and thin.

"What made you decide to start a business in consumer lending? Why should I give you my money?"

"We know many people coming out of college and also people who have failed or are about to fail in business not being able to obtain continued financing."

"Whoa! I'm going to stop you right there. Why continue financing something that is not currently working. If the business model doesn't work, why continue to burn more cash?" Sharon sees her advocate questioning as a red light already.

"In some instances, more time is needed. In others, starting a whole new business model after closing doors is too expensive. A lot of money can be saved by quickly changing products, services, and target market with the same business," says James.

"Consumer lending is difficult due to managing all the account receivables. We know these are consumers with bad credit. That's why we have two installments in the lending program. If the first installment is not paid back with continued payments, we keep the second installment of the program as collateral," says Griffin as if explaining a bright idea.

Now Griffin and James have come to the negotiating stage in terms of how much equity Sharon is willing to invest. Silence draws on once again. Numbers, analysis, and calculations are running through Sharon's mind as if being flashed on a computer screen in front of her. Griffin gives James a nudge to let him know the deal is about to conclude.

"We are asking for one hundred grand for a thirty-three percent stake in our business," says Griffin with all the confidence he could while making eye contact with Sharon.

"I have been in this business for twenty years, just after divorcing my second husband is when it began. You have my consent, as I'm content with your terms. If you do not live up to your terms, they become my terms."

"How much debt to equity do we have now Griffin," says James looking up at the light fixture above him.

"The debt to equity ratio is two to one," says Griffin under his breath.

"That's too much debt, what are the payments per month and what is the fixed rate of interest?"

"We need customers, we need customers Griffin!" says James enthusiastically.

"Instead of being in business to make a profit, we need to be in business to get and keep customers," says Griffin.

Getting back to James's previous question, "the monthly payment is eighteen grand roughly and interest is five percent."

Griffin and James are burning the midnight oil; it's two in the morning, dark circles under both their eyes on a Sunday night. The business suite they have been renting is in a busy neighborhood of the city with rent costing three grand per month. A spreadsheet on a computer shows Griffin the balance sheet for Dynamic Lenders. A picture of Albert Einstein sticking his tongue out hangs on the wall next to a digital clock. On the other side of the room, there is a copy of Vincent van Gogh's *The Starry Night* along with a copy of Marc Chagall's *Job in Despair*. All these people are here as a motley crew overlooking them for offering guidance in their endeavors.

A scientist and two artists are formed to become a part of the glorified culture of the Dynamic Lenders business. There is no employee of the month to hang up on the bulletin board. There is just a fellowship formed by the owners consisting of a scientist and two artists, which at one point in their lives were told they could not do something and defied the difficulty.

Next to the computer screen is Barron's Business Dictionary and Stigum's Money Market books. They belong to James, who believes more in calculating words than charismatic vision. The coffee pot next to the restroom door is on again for the fourth time that night. James stands half asleep waiting for the dripping coffee to slow down to fill his empty cup.

"Hep, hep, hoyt, that's the money maker my friend," says Griffin having something in his vision click for the first time in the last hour and a half. "There's the big Monday night game tomorrow. There's a street fair downtown, and next weekend we have a booth at the trade show in Bennigan's Arena. What do you say?"

"That's a start to get our name out there. I get dibs on running the spin wheel for prize drawing at the trade show," says James taking a big sip of freshly made brew.

"Knock yourself out, I feel like jumping in the spin wheel running in place. If only our spin wheel was life size huh?"

✎

"We offer personal loans with bad credit and no background check required," says James.

"My name is Tony, I have to pay my rent, but my credit card is maxed out and my wages are garnished due to tax fraud. What terms can I get?"

"How much do you need?"

"I need seven hundred dollars," says Tony looking down disappointed.

"At that amount, I can lend at twenty-two percent APR. Stop by our office location to see your options for repayment."

"What is your best option?"

"We have an extended payment plan where you pay more over the life of the loan. In the regular payment plan, no interest accrues in the first two months. Over fourteen hundred dollars will be the total paid over the life of the loan."

Another person approaches the booth while Tony is looking at a free brochure. One look at the name, Dynamic Lenders, and his thick eyebrows raise on his forehead with skepticism. Wearing kaki shorts and a black Harley Davidson t-shirt, his black hair in a ponytail matches his sun glasses resting on his forehead.

"What do you do?" asks the man in the Harley shirt.

"We lend consumer and business loans," says James.

"I have a brother who borrowed a grand to make a car repair and ended up paying a total of four grand over the life of the loan. That ruined our summer vacation plans and he had to get a second job to pay off the mountain of interest that was accruing."

"Our business gives immediate access to money when one cannot get it elsewhere. The value of creating convenient access to money is going to have a high price. Your brother got his money for the repair and paid the market value for getting his problem solved in his situation," says James.

"Whatever, you guys are a rip-off," says the man in a Harley shirt before walking away.

Tony kept the brochure and moved on to next booth. As the day progressed, more and more people entered the packed arena, the booth did a great job of promoting and spreading word from person to person about the Dynamic Lenders business James and Griffin started. Next month's lending increased dramatically with the end of the month pinch most consumers feel when running out of money to pay their bills.

## WALKING OUT

The TV in the office is broadcasting a game show, the contestant has just made a big risk and it paid off. However, the contestant has to make an even bigger risk to keep going. The anticipation to win even bigger looms heavily on the contestant's shoulders. If only they knew the low odds of winning if they keep going. The contestant gives it another try and loses the big cash prize, going home with nine-hundred dollars.

The situation on TV compared to the situation with Griffin and James's lending business is similar. Both have continually made high risks to the point of not being able to go on anymore. This is now an office with the atmosphere of pity and a culture of regret. Where did this all go wrong? Whose fault is it? They have risked all and are rewarded with nothing.

"What are you doing?" says Griffin watching James pack his things. "You're leaving me. Don't give up on this, don't do this."

"It was never going to work Griffin."

"You are saying this in the past tense, which means you've doubted our business all along."

"Yep, it was a brilliant idea. Perhaps, too brilliant for anyone to understand it, you need to know when to quit. Passion and pride have made us delusional."

"You're being negative and pessimistic."

"No, I'm being realistic and practical. I see myself as a realist, right here and right now. I see things for what they actually are, not what I want them to be. You're version of optimism is a world full of rainbows and unicorns."

James lifts his box of belongings from his desk and almost loses his big bowling trophy. He has to side step to balance the equilibrium of the objects in the box. Griffin looks up at the lights, which are not on due to not paying the electric bill. Even without utilities, he refuses to register the fact that the business is going under and smiles like he's about to blow out birthday candles. James walks towards the front door.

"You're sure you want to leave."

"I'm out man, see ya," says James using the remote to turn off the TV and walking out the front door not looking back.

Silence fills the room where Griffin is the only remaining partner in a struggling business. He looks out the window in a daze, completely unaware of his surroundings as he continues to use his charisma to see a solution of meeting business expenses this month.

✑

A week later, James is lying on a sofa looking up at the ceiling of a psychiatrist office. Deciding to see a shrink is a way for James to reflect and move forward with his problems. Psychological analysis allows him to see a solution through reflecting. The Psychiatrist's name is Dianne, a heavy set woman in her forties with brown hair and old fashioned black rimmed glasses sitting at edge of her nose as she looks down at her notes. Her office has no walls; the walls are bookshelves as tall as the ceiling.

"How can I do better?" asks James.

"You can't do better, what else is there for you to do?" asks Dianne

"There's always room to do better, don't you see it?"

"I think you see it as a never ending process. Does it ever stop for you? Does it ever come to an end?"

"No not really. Work hard, play hard is my mantra."

"What is it that you are doing anyway?"

"I watch things grow."

"You watch things grow, what do you watch grow?"

"Everything, everything I touch I want it to turn to gold. I want to gild everything. Interestingly, I watch one thing in relation to another in cause and effect."

"Do you like to watch things grow? If so, what do you like to watch grow?" asks Dianne repeating her question.

"Yeah, I'm most interested in inventions and the value of money. I'm not interested in people growing, just processes and tasks. People are flawed, their guided with subjective feelings and emotions. A supply chain managing more and more inventory or a fast-food pizza place building new locations across the nation, that is the growth I like."

"Sounds like an entrepreneur."

"You're right, you're exactly right. You see, I'm obsessed with the idea of the multiplier effect, which I learned in college."

"Funny how one term definition can grab a person and motivate them so much, I say ideology and philosophy makes it so."

*

Griffin is sitting at the desk of his bank's loan officer, Hattie. There are old black and white photos hanging on the wall, old photos from the early twentieth century. None of them have people just landscapes of farmsteads, rural main streets, and old cars with flat tires and broken windows.

"There's too much debt, way too much debt!!!" says Hattie with concern.

"Well, I had to pay the bills and make payroll last month," says Griffin.

"Debt should be no more than a half of the total capital of your business. Debt is death; you can die from it like a snare. Have lean finances and a lot these problems you're having won't occur."

"How many employees do you have?"

"Two…well one now because my partner walked out the other day."

"That should help you to create more efficiency."

"What about the customers and their families? This loan program helps to make their operations run smoothly."

"The way I look at it they won't have a job if this keeps going on to where you're paying off debt with debt. You can't keep pushing the can down the road. I have already looked at your balance statement and said this is too risky."

"What can I do? What are my options?"

"Sell the loans making the least amount of money, sell part of the business to gain more working capital…"

"You mean take on a partner, I'll lose control of the business; especially if I sell half."

"Also, consolidate debt into one source, which is more difficult when working with freelance lenders. Try to bring in more revenue by changing your business model or what you offer to customers. Create an alliance with another business to funnel your customers into complimentary offerings of products and services."

"Look this all seems great, but…"

"But what, look, you can ignore the options I'm giving you or you can try to apply them to save your business in the long run. Look you can always go out of business and since your setup as a limited liability company; you're not personally liable for default on your loans. Try to get a big buyer to help you out."

☙

At Griffin's apartment, Lara is having iced tea watching the latest episode of *The Bachelor*. She lies on the couch and gets interested in the gossip and false rumors the contestants are saying about each other, very entertaining. Lara is exhausted after her girls' night out with friends. Griffin sits in his recliner reading through his e-mails on his smartphone. He is not looking forward to Monday morning when having to face the details of his zombie business with no cash flow. The apartment is old, with the flooring, carpet, and patio door all needing to be replaced.

"Your greed is choking me, I want to live life sometime in the near future," says Lara upset with Griffin over length of time his business is taking to generate a profit. Having no money is an aspect of an entrepreneur's lifestyle.

"We will honey, we'll go on vacation next summer. I'm still in the process of liquidating the assets from my partnership with James," says Griffin with an understanding that they haven't had much time together in last couple of years.

"We will go on vacation next year. I will hold you accountable you know. Don't play politics by telling me what I want to hear. An individual participates in politics with deceit. Pretending to understand the other's opinion, when actually one does not and only holds their ignorance in check. They lie about commitments, values, and beliefs in order to support others and make their position in society more favorable."

"They're not pretending to understand another's opinion, their own opinion and self-interest is more important to them."

"See what I mean, you understand what you're doing, you even corrected me."

"Look my word is my word okay. When I get settled into my next job, we'll go on vacation to Hawaii."

Lara goes into the bedroom and puts on a Hawaiian shirt and sun glasses. She rubs sun screen on her face, arms, and legs and goes out the patio door to sit in the sun on the deck.

# HANK HAWK

"I'm getting out of this business as well James. Yeah good bye, sayonara. I'll be in on Monday to take the last of my office supplies out of the office," says Griffin on the phone with James.

All that is left are the computers, phones, chairs, filing cabinets, and desk lights to be removed. The time is ten in the evening and Griffin's eyes are tired and he can't seem to drink enough water to stay hydrated. All the caffeine in his body is acting like a diuretic. A light above the entrance door and above his office desk are the only two lights on being battery operated. The office area has five cubicle spaces with a front desk for the customer service representative. The office area is in a strip mall along a growing development in Baltimore.

James responds to Griffin's fair well. "Okay, just drop the key off at the office on Monday. I really thought we had a great set up at the start. I've seen businesses start out a lot worse and still make it."

"Please don't compare us to others. We don't compare to others James," says Griffin with an angry voice over the phone.

"The business has encountered some problems. I plan to spend time in this mess of problems to find valuable learning opportunities in the trenches. I hope to make sure this never happens again."

"I'm out James; I don't need to sit in the trenches to learn from this bleak situation. You can run the numbers and get calculations all you want. However, some things you cannot measure like intangibles." Switching to sarcasm in his voice he jokingly says. "It's a coincidence that the name was Dynamic Lenders, it expresses our weakness not our strength. With too many variables to consider, the onslaught of variables in the business model created too many complicated calculations for you and you walked out and quit."

"Sorry, I just want to say, I wish you the best in the future."

Griffin is the first to hang up the phone to end the conversation.

The night club is dark with orange light radiating off of wall lights above the half-moon shaped bar tables with leather upholstered seats. Three games of pool are being played by young gentlemen in business suits with ties hanging loose around their necks at one end of the club and exotic dancers are performing on stage at the other end. The bar is located in the center of the night club with a circular bar and three bartenders, two females and one male mixing drinks. Three waitresses are busy serving and cleaning tables and shot glasses. The big man in the club is Hank Hawk, who is clearly drawing the most attention with the biggest booth next to the stage of dancers. Three women and five men sit with him. He has a mustache and long black hair pulled back in a ponytail. At 5 foot 10, his small frame consists of one hundred and eighty pounds. Hank talks confidently under his breath to the man seated across from him.

"Who's better, Johnny at negotiating a contract or Jared at telling the truth to his wife about if she looks fat in this evening's dress?" says Hank with a chuckle at his own mockery.

"Definitely Johnny because Jared's answer to his wife is never the right answer, not a good outcome to have," says Francis in a red and black suit.

"Well, well, well, what is this?" says Hank being approached by Griffin wearing a white dress shirt and black vest and tie.

"I'm looking for an angel investor and I've been told you can help. My name is Griffin by the way."

"Nice to meet you Griffin, what type of business are we talking about?" says Hank rotating a nice championship ring on his finger, diamonds shining in the lights.

Hank clearly has an ancestry blood line from Spain or Italy and his cuisine matches with Mediterranean fish and salad steaming up from the plate in front of him. The brunette sitting next to him fixes her eyes on him all the time showing an affectionate facial expression. She seems to be always smiling and flirting without words, she inhales her cigarette in brief puffs. Her long sleeve gloves match her golden shaded dress. Hank is clearly a person who has the world by the ass.

"The business is an invention think tank, and a great vertical integration generator."

"I've heard it all Griffin. How much do you need?"

"Four hundred grand."

"How much do you want? Four hundred grand?"

"About double that would be nice."

"Well, I can do both because I'm a man that goes with the flow. You see this championship ring on my finger. This is from winning the 1988 College Baseball World Series. I played third base or 'hot box' they called it. When fielding a ball you definitely had to be on your toes, you had to be 'in the zone'; you would go with the flow of the experience without thinking about reactions. A ball player has to know what they are going to do with ball before they get it or otherwise the opponent will seize opportunities and score."

"I can honestly say I'm "in the zone" and have that sense of flow with this business venture Hank."

"I'm going to cut you a deal, here is my partner Mr. Winthrop. Here is his card and he will be ready with capital in a month. I like you kid, I like the engagement you have with this business idea. Your relationship with this idea is intrinsic; I hope the marketing goes okay for you."

"I appreciate your generous investment and assure you the money will be put to good use," says Griffin taking a business card with Mr. Winthrop's contact information on it.

The woman on Hank's right is older than Hank with a black dress and black hair. She wears her hair down to faintly cover the big diamond earrings. The focus of her attention this entire time has been at the dance floor some fifty feet away. Her attention was definitely in another world as if day dreaming. She is the opposite type of personality from the brunette on Hank's left.

"Griffin, I'd like you to meet my sister Ellen Johnson," Hank moves his hands and eyes to the day dreaming woman to his right. She comes back to focus and looks at Griffin.

"Yes, Griffin I wish you luck on your venture. Go get em," Ellen smiles to show the most symmetrically white teeth possible.

"And this is my wife Hillary," Hank says moving his thumbs and eyes to his left at the brunette. Hillary smiles wider now with closed lips and squinting eyes.

"Nice to meet you Griffin. How do you plan to grow your business?" asks Hillary.

Griffin pauses for five seconds to decide on a response. "Well, you saw the patent office make their money from patent fees. I will charge a fee for studio space or a fee for the profits my tenants or "thinkers" generate with their inventions."

"What is the difference?" says Hillary rolling her eyes up to the ceiling to show her thoughts of this being a lame idea.

"Some people want just working space, so I will provide that. On the other hand, some people want capital and a working team for their idea or product and I can provide that as well. Imagine a group of computer geeks given freedom to do what they wanted to with sufficient resources. Something is bound to happen, and I bet in today's world it will be remarkable."

"So your plan is to provide people with resources to bring their inventions to reality. This is similar to Hank here putting forth the money to start your business," says Hillary trying to gesture her hand to bring Hank back into the conversation.

"A domino effect, will the effect continue forever?" says Hank with curiosity.

"I'm just a supplier looking to make a profit by adding another step in the business startup. Look here, banks are not loaning entrepreneurs money all of the time. There are a lot of ideas that do not come to fruition due to lack of resources. This business is necessary and is needed," says Griffin.

"Lack of resources and knowledge I might add. What about the last business venture you failed at Griffin?" says Hank with a grinning smile as being curious to what Griffin will say.

"That was just a character builder for me. I will find my true self, capabilities, and character when looking into the abyss. I crave for the need to live on the edge and smile in the face of adversity."

"You should celebrate now Griffin, hit the dance floor over there with them pretty ladies," says Ellen moving her eyes over to the dance floor she was just looking at and day dreaming moments before.

"Again thank you Hank," says Griffin shaking Hank's hand in a firm grip.

Griffin stands up, slides his chair into the table, and walks past the dining tables to the dance floor where a crowd of about thirty people dance to hip hop music. The exotic dancers are next to the DJ music player with sparkling lingerie and performing a dance routine. Griffin goes over to a couple of women talking at the edge of the dance floor.

"Hi my name is Griffin, I'm looking to see if you would care for a dance," says Griffin giving a stare into the lady's eyes, she has blond hair wearing a red blouse and blue jeans.

Griffin loosens his black neck tie and puts his hands interlocked behind the back. Waiting to see if the blond lady responds to the invitation. Lara extends out her hand to Griffin.

"My name is Lara," says Lara trying to be spontaneous and walking with Griffin to an open space on the dance floor.

The two hold each other closely hand in hand, dancing to rhythmic hip hop music. The next song is techno with Griffin and Lara having more distance between each other. They break dance, Lara showing fluency and finesse and Griffin showing inflexible robotic movements. Lara looks on with wide eyed wonder about where Griffin gets the dances he's doing. After the song ends, the rhythmic movements to the songs beat begins fade away. Being taller than Lara, Griffin's looks down into her eyes as they dance slowly while close to each other. They take small steps in a circular motion and Griffin changes his hands on Lara from her waist to his right hand at the small of her back, his left hand holds her right hand at shoulder level.

Griffin and Lara change to a side step in a circular motion. They move in the opposite direction of the spinning disco ball on the ceiling to make them seem to move faster than they actually are. Lara starts to crack a smile and openly laughs as Griffin almost stumbles over his feet.

"I would have never thought I could dance like this. Is it because of you or me? I think you are up to it," says Griffin.

"It's all you Griffin; I'm just riding along in the side car," says Lara.

The music song next is Chris Young's, "Who I am with You". The lights become dim and Griffin and Lara slow their dancing to the beat of the music. Shifting their stare from eye to eye reading each other's thoughts, Griffin kisses Lara on the forehead.

"You missed," says Lara biting her lower lip.

Even in the dim lights, Lara's blond hair shows bright in the moving lights coming from the disco ball. The ball room dance floor is now packed with only half the dining tables being filled now. Griffin licks his lips and then purses them before meeting Lara half way for a kiss.

"Did I miss that time?" asks Griffin.

"Right on, double or nothing, what do you say, try again?" says Lara with a glowing facial expression with a smile.

The two kiss again, this time for a longer period…

## LEARNING LECTURE

Griffin is sitting in his 1971 Plymouth Cuda convertible on a mid-morning Friday outside his bank. The collectible car is red with white rear fenders, a black hood scoop, and tan leather seats. He sits talking on the speaker phone connected to blue tooth. The sun reflects off the newly waxed car body, which makes the red reflect from the hood through the windshield glass into Griffin's eyes. The new applicant to the business incubator is a young woman online merchant looking to be a low cost provider of cosmetics.

"We have a space at $200 per month for your business," says Griffin trying to block the sun's reflection through the windshield.

"Great, when can I move in?" asks Marissa.

"Next month the space will be ready, just call me and we will give you the keys after signing the lease agreement. Yep, the application has been approved and back ground check cleared," says Griffin looking to end the conversation to make it to his eleven o'clock appointment with Hattie, his Loan Officer. "What drives you to go into business for yourself?"

"I think I can do business better than anyone out there. I grew up in a middle class family and went to college not realizing the amount of money I was paying and taking on credit card debt. Two years after graduating, I worked three jobs and looking to start my own business for the chance of being rewarded for the risks being taken."

"You remind me of myself enjoying games of chance. My first business attempt failed with my partner and now I'm looking to start fresh as a landlord. I got to go Marissa, bye."

Griffin walks into the bank and waits in Hattie's office. During the wait he can over hear a conversation taking place in a room close by. A man is talking to Hattie, just finishing up a previous appointment.

"Risk, now that's a topic with varying opinions and opposing viewpoints. This bank's process for approving loan applications is objective and an equal opportunity."

The man turns hysterical to let loose his frustration of being denied a loan. "Yes, I have debts that need to be paid back. The loans are in my name. They're all mine you see. No one else wants them and no one else can have them. I have the privilege of ridding myself of my own debt. I'm different from others by not having to figure out what next to get in the process of pursuing the American Dream. I run on fumes, and so frugal that I don't want to eat sometimes."

The man walks out of the office towards the entrance, he catches a hold of his loose hysterical emotions and brings it under control. The man wears a blue polo shirt, kakis, blond hair, mustache, and low reaching side burns. After a moment, Hattie walks in with a surprising look from the cynicism of the previous appointment. Another woman enters the office room and sits in the wooden chair with cushions and arm rests next to Hattie. With a pen holding her hair up, the woman is taller than Hattie by six inches, red hair, and smiling with dimples on her cheeks.

"Hi, my name is Kathy, a financial advisor here at the bank. Griffin, how much debt do you have from your last business venture?" says Kathy sitting cross legged wearing a black skirt, leggings, and a white dress shirt.

"Ah, about forty grand is remaining."

"I advise a person to get rid of that debt before taking on any additional debt. When the previous debt is eliminated, then the time is right to take out another business loan. I see there to be three hundred and twenty grand on the balance sheet of the Business Incubator.

That's odd, you named the business what it is literally?" asks Kathy.

"I did that approach with naming my dog, Dog. Pretty straight forward, nothing fancy, simple, it's what it is," says Griffin.

"The time frame for Griffin is short-term and timing may never be right, therefore the best time is right now," says Hattie.

"Anyway, out of college I was not able to get the job I wanted, so I went into business for myself. My plan did not work, but at least I'm trying," says Griffin trying to get out of the topic of discussion.

"That's the right mind set in business, don't be afraid to fail," says Hattie.

"I'm more concerned about the people I'm going into business with than about failing. Last time, my partner bailed on me when the business cycle was down," says Griffin.

"Great point about relationships in business making or breaking you. The devil can be in disguise. Careful because the wolf can wear the hide of a sheep, or a lion can be amongst sheep," says Kathy trying to provide a lesson learned ahead of time.

"I think importance must be placed on a person having the view of every person being a great person until proven otherwise, giving the benefit of the doubt," says Hattie.

"Sir, my advice is you will never make it. This idea of additional debt is preposterous," says Kathy changing to a negative attitude about the matter at hand.

"Yeah, like I haven't heard that before," says Griffin.

"Sir, we cannot approve for an additional line of credit for your business. Your going to ruin the business without getting the property fully leased out," says Kathy.

"Well, what should I do?"

"You should try getting a job at Bankowski's Law Firm."

"Bankowski's, everything there is an act of congress; it takes them a year for what it takes me to do in two months. My own company is more flexible and quicker at making decisions and changes."

"If this business fails, you will be in financial ruin; your debts could only be forgiven in bankruptcy. Your credit score will be tarnished for a decade."

"I have established an LLC so the company's finances will not be linked to my own."

Everyone is silent for a minute as a pause is taken to think of additional thoughts for continued discussion.

"Your right this is a huge risk I'm taking. In other words, there is no reward without risk when it comes to business. What do you say if I risk twenty percent of my finances for the company to go extreme?" says Griffin.

"Fair enough, I suppose you're less likely to lose it all. Your business has very little revenue currently. How can you possibly get a consistent revenue going?" asks Kathy.

"Yes, business is slow right now; I need tenants, tenants who will stay for at least three years at time before moving out."

"How will you take on the first and second round of financing, it's impossible?" asks Hattie.

"When business becomes consistent, I will. I look for ways to attract tenants and it's the launch requiring the most effort and financing."

"You're flirting with failure and will not be able to compete with the big boys."

"I've been beat up by the big boys and playing this game for some time. I know what I need to do to make it. This all comes down to rice and beans on a shoestring budget. Right now, I'm standing ten inches in my own shit. I'm standing in it and I would not want to be anywhere else."

# TWENTY YEARS EARLIER

"He wouldn't hurt a fly," Mother said to the preschool teacher, speaking about her son James.

WHACK!, a big slap came from a fly swatter hitting the flat surface of the kitchen table. The lanky boy has a surprised look on his face from actually getting the fly. He thought his chances were very low on getting the fly; since the fly clearly noticed him sneaking up to him in the first place. James did not know the key to getting the fly was the holes in the fly swatter confusing the fly's vision, which made the fly think there was no harm from the object coming towards it.

"I got it!"

"James, can you come here? I need you to do something for Mrs. Jolenheim," said Mother.

Mother has black hair and a red dress she used to wear while waitressing at the local truck stop on Interstate 95 on the outskirts of Baltimore. Mrs. Jolenheim is a tall blond in her forties and towering figure over little

James. Her bright red lipstick makes her dark red shirt contrast. The boy is almost intimidated when she stands up to get her supplies from her carrying bag.

Mrs. Jolenheim was busy at work preparing a test for James detailing shapes and there relations to everyday objects, such as circles and the moon, squares and an ice cube, and rectangle and a door. Putting all her attention into assembling the test, she lost track of time. The 60 seconds it took to pull the diagram out of her carrying bag of supplies and assemble the pieces in a disorganized way, spread out on the table.

"OK, James can you match the shapes onto the picture? See the circle fitting in with the moon and the sun. What other pictures does the circle fit into? Can you show me?"

"Yep, here," He takes the rectangle pieces and arranges them into a big rectangle on the diagram.

A look of disappointment shows on Mom's face. She knows James can do better than this to fulfill Mrs. Jolenheim's request.

# FIFTEEN YEARS LATER

Sitting in a lecture hall of Wharton's Business School, the large white sound panels taking away the echoes protrude three inches from the wall. A fluorescent light above flickers on and off and constantly buzzes like a bug zapper. Two young adults sit in the front row, while the majority of the students have packed the top row, in the back of the stadium seating.

Professor Giottson is a man in his fifties with black hair gelled and combed back. His red tie is pinched under the Windsor knot, a mark that he has excellent Windsor knot tying skills. He stands behind his podium looking down at his notes and daily planner. He never reads from the textbook, that is for the students to do, his job is to add to the textbook and explain further, applying the theories and lessons in examples.

The two in the front row are James and a young lady named Stacy with brunette hair down to her shoulders and bangs tucked behind her ear. James wears a red hoody sweat shirt and black jeans, glasses rest at the tip of his nose as he looks down taking notes. Stacy wears her good luck charm bracelet on her left wrist and her purse is tucked between her and the arm rest of her student seat. Typing away on her laptop, she takes notes the proper way with roman numerals for main sections and sub-categories for each section. She wears Dupree style jeans and an orange coat due to the room being cold all the time.

"Why does the Central Bank lower interest rate?" asks Professor Giottson.

"Low interest rates are supposed to help the finance industry lend more loans," says Stacy in the front row.

"Have you ever heard of Pareto's Law 80/20 Principle?" The students are speechless, even the ones who read the assigned chapters over the weekend. Pareto's Law is not in the textbook.

"No?" questions Professor Giottson. "Well, it entails that twenty percent of work, which is equal to time or effort gets most of results."

"Tit for Tat what is that? Did anybody do their assigned reading over the weekend?"

"A strategy of reciprocity by matching opponent's moves," says Stacy again.

"Who can give me examples of Tit for Tat being used in the real world?" A thirty second pause of silence with no students voluntarily answering. "We're dead in the water again. The water is going down and the rocks are showing."

"To those who hate college classes, I have some advice for you. You will have to study your whole life, your future employers don't care about your personal problems, and there are no rewards for working extra. Now where were we?"

"Ping pong and the Cold War with Russia," says James giving an analogy of Tit for Tat.

"A husband and wife settle a divorce in court," says a young man in the back row.

"A car buyer and a sales person negotiating a sales price."

"An auction where two bidders bid for the purchase of a famous Renaissance Painting."

"Good, those are all good examples. Now, with only ten minutes left of class are there any other questions?" asks the Professor.

"Professor, everyone seems to be focused on return on investment, however a large factor is principle of the investment and how that is related to ROI. What is more important the return or the principle?" asks James.

"That is a good question; let's say the average annual return on an investment is seven percent. Now, a rate of return of twenty, thirty, or even two-hundred percent could happen, but with less probability. We also know that this return is not sustainable and is volatile. The great industrialists who built America in the 19th and 20th centuries were focused on one thing. My opinion is that one thing was saving money and reducing costs to be able to do more with their capital. Principle was made up of every penny being tracked and recorded in their ledger; this is a very detailed and thorough process. One of my biggest pet peeves is seeing an individual throw their pocket change in the garbage. The lean manufacturing proclaimed by Toyota in the 1980's is not a totally new process. The successful industrialist owners of the 19th century were thinking in similar terms. Even civilizations centuries before us were very picky about their financial records. Using economies of scale to having savings per unit reduced is also a way to produce more with less. To your point on principle: $10,000 x 1.07%= $10,700 and twenty grand would have doubled the return to $21,400. All in all you need more money to make more money. If you can increase your amount of principle investment by reducing costs and recording every penny, do it."

"Professor, I will ask you again. Yes or no? Is principle more important than rate of return in an investment?" asks James again.

"Yes, shall I continue? The amount of principle invested is the one thing a person has total control over. The rate of return is complex and depends on many variables influencing it at any given time. The rate of return is not in the investors control like the original amount of principle is. However, there is a possibility of having a negative rate of return and principle goes down in value."

The class ends and the students leave the lecture hall.

# "MAN MEETS WOMAN"

**Five Years Later**

"I like to keep good tabs on my collection. Perhaps, I will stop being so obsessed some day. Can you help me help myself?" asks Griffin to the waiter at the luxurious Gwen's Restaurant.

"Help me help myself? Over what do you speak of? This obsession you speak of please describe in detail," says the waiter a tall lanky man in a black tailor suit.

"Business of course; son, have you ever went to the lengths of work to make your head hurt? This is the point where a person's eyes burn and the heart palpates out of control."

"No, sir. Are you talking about physical and mental tiredness, a nervous breakdown? Are you ready to order?"

"Yes, I will take the Walleye Stir Fry and a glass of 18th century French wine," says Griffin looking over at another waiter serving the table next to him with a family of five."

"Great choice sir and I wish you the best with your business work," says the waiter bowing his head down before he leaves.

Looking around, Griffin is the only person in the restaurant dining by himself. The white table cloth in front of him matches the white painted walls, ceiling, chairs, and doors. The carpet is green along with the light shades to make a bright and dark green color radiate through the entire dining area. Quietness is the niche and a unique aspect at Gwen's. Everyone is relaxed and the best method for Griffin to keep from falling asleep is to fidget his fingers.

"Here we go sir. Careful the plate is hot, and the wine, among the best grape vines in the hills of France."

"That was quick; I hope to have a great way to have your quickness in my business. Great sense of urgency, diligence, making the customer number one. Waiter, or may I call you Waiter?"

The waiter responds after pouring the wine into the wine glass. "My name is Aden, is there anything I can do for you sir?" asks Aden.

"I'm looking for the bill to be split into two. As soon as I'm finished with my meal there will be a meeting with a friend, hold my bill until after the meeting will you?"

"Yes, can do sir."

Griffin takes his time to eat the stir fry and finishes the wine before the meal. Aden picks up the finished plates and has a great way of collecting the massive dishes to carry to the back prepping area. A tall man at six-four walks through the dining tables to sit across the table from Aden. His black archaeology hat and gray overcoat fit him very loosely. He has a goatee, thick sideburns of black hair, and brown eyes. His nose is big, too pointy with big boned cheeks.

"Welcome Harry, good to see you could make it."

"Griffin," Harry tips his hat down with his index finger to give Griffin a nod of recognition, "How is business?" asks Harry unbuttoning his brown overcoat to reveal a dark green vest and white dress shirt underneath.

"Business is starting, but I'm in a real pickle on this one. Do you have any ideas?"

"What is your number of vacant spaces? To succeed, you need a way to funnel in tenants."

"I'm working closely with area colleges, tech companies, and the financial intermediaries."

"That is a good start, consider arts, medical, and judicial routes too. Creativity is great for ideas; it's amazing what an artist can do from humble beginnings. Medical advancements will build capital easily, and judicial laws based on moral philosophies are the greatest knowledge between what is legal and illegal, and of course, all the loop holes in between."

The two men become silent looking down at the table between them. They dawn on the endless possibilities for Griffin's Business Incubator.

"I'm also here to present a proposal to you Harry, seeing if Luxington Gibbons will accept."

Harry smirks not sure what he will hear from Griffin next.

"Your work is in getting the impossible made possible. Harry, I need an additional round of financing to stay afloat. Can you find a private investor? If I get more office space leased, can you manage getting more equity or debt?" asks Griffin.

"Of course, I will need to know what the rating is on occupancy turnover and... you know the numbers investors care about when making risk/ reward calculations. Luxington Gibbons might buy five hundred bonds to be purchased by his investment company."

"Wow, this is a potential deal I cannot refuse," says Griffin.

"One more thing, you need to cover my bill tonight, not much, just eighty dollars worth."

Harry looks staring into Griffin's facial expression. Twenty seconds go by where both are seated silent without an action or change of expression. Harry takes his thoughts into a different realm while Griffin is concentrated on the family of five seated next to him.

"Business looks to be starting good, how's your lady been, Griffin?" asks Harry.

"I've been holding off on starting a family, you see I just can't pursue it. If I were to pursue it, I would be pursuing it with vengeance. I would be pursuing the American dream and my lofty goals with a vengeance."

"Or you could say their lofty goals under a compromise," says Harry as if he's experienced marital conflict before.

"Anyway, let's stick to business. Here's the deal for the public, there will be 3 million dollars of convertible bonds available. If the company can get eight to twelve fixed income investors that would be great."

"Sounds great, I will fax over the documents for debt issuance of the underwriting process tomorrow morning. Oh, by the way don't be afraid to live life to the fullest once in your personal life. You're dammed if you do and dammed if you don't," says Harry.

Aden comes by quickly on his way to the table to drop off the two separate bills.

"Thanks a plenty," says Griffin shaking Harry's hand while standing next to him seated at the table.

Harry turns opens the leather bill cover and see's his twenty dollar wine and appetizer bill with Griffin's eighty dollar tally. "Oh my, the man is sure is asking a lot," says Harry whispering to himself.

Griffin has left the dining area with Harry having Aden take the payment. Upon Aden's return with the receipt, Harry can not help but look at the young man with a gesture of the bright future he has ahead of him. Of course, Aden takes the gesture for granted and can not figure out why Harry thinks that way at all.

*✒*

The next day, Griffin is out shopping in the grocery store when he sees a familiar face grabbing yogurt from the fridge in the dairy section. The person is an acquaintance from a long time ago.

"Erin, is that you?" says Griffin.

"Oh my God, Griffin! It's so good to see you, how have you been?" says Erin with a look of amazement on her face.

Griffin wears a green long sleeve turtle neck sweatshirt with blue jeans. Erin is a brunette and is fully accessorized from head to toe; her flannel over coat, red shirt and skirt matches her high heels and glossed lips.

"I've been great…It's been what? Fifteen years now."

"Yep, back in the day I remember you had long hair, but now I don't even recognize you."

"Remember the time when we went fishing and I hooked your ear when casting my line?" says Griffin.

"Yeah, that hurt so bad. I still have a scar. Say, do you have any kids?" asks Erin.

"Do I have the qualifications to be a family man? To be a loving husband and father, am I good enough?"

"You shouldn't be so hard on yourself. Yes, I'm sure you have the qualifications."

"Ah, no worries, I'm young yet. I have fifteen years."

"Yeah, that's right you are young yet."

"In fifteen years, my worries will be replaced with regret by not having lived life to the fullest."

"Well, great seeing you Griffin. I have to go, take care," says Erin waving a good bye.

Sitting in Dianne's psychiatrist's office, the sunlight shines bright through the windows. A repetitive ticking occurs like a clock. Only it's not a clock it's a Newton's

Cradle swinging back and forth. The metronome cadence is like a tempo making the mind travel a guided road of hypnosis. The mind is in a daze after spending an hour in this office with the repetitive tempo.

The unwritten and unsaid rule is to not say anything, just observe the thoughts in your mind. Memories, reflections, emotions, feelings, and observations, most of life is spent in this form, just doing tasks and learning through observation. Trial and error makes the discovery experience. Speechless, the person with a good vocabulary would be able to describe what is going on with great detail. However, the ability to do this is limited by an individual's inability to take an experience all in at once. Perhaps, thousands of people should experience the same event and explain what they saw in detail to obtain the most out of the experience.

Another point of view is the observation's accuracy, which could be delusional. The person sees what they want to see or there is a subjective biased influenced by their feelings or emotions. Objective observation requires sanity and an individual having their psychological bearings.

"What have you been up to?" asks Psychiatrist Dianne Dixon.

"I've been goin to the gym lately. I keep a journal how the workout goes, how I feel and what not," says James.

"Good, what do you journal about?"

James opens up his journal to the page that is bookmarked. "I write the following:"

*Day 1: I'm excited today, to be starting a journey of working on myself to improve, to have "me" time. Half way through the workout I'm exhausted, my limbs are dead tired and heavy from lifting weights. I'm light headed and feel like I'm going to pass out or faint or something.*

*Day 2: I'm back at it again, this time starting with less energy than before. I had to convince myself that I like working out. There is definitely an award I feel after the workouts than before I start.*

*Day 3: My muscles are sore; every time I move during my day I'm reminded of how sore I am. I now think I go to the gym to torture myself; however, when my conditioning improves I will not be as sore. There is a difference between being sore and being injured my high school coach used to say. Soreness lasts less than a week, if you're still in pain for more than a week it's an injury.*

*Day 4: I almost didn't make it to the gym today; I had to drag myself to get here. This experience is definitely mind over body as they say. Each set of ten reps is a trial of exhaustion and suffering tiredness. Two minutes later, I'm fully recovered and do another set to feel even more tired.*

*Day 5: Today, I'm here but I'm not here. My body is here and my mind is elsewhere such as, at work, at home, or what I'm going to eat for dinner. My workout plan was to do free weight squats, but all the squat racks are occupied by others and I'm not willing to wait for the individuals to finish. Instead, I head to the seated leg press and do my sets there. My legs are tired after the first set. I have to remind myself the tiredness is temporary. I reach the point of threshold on my third set and*

> *my leg muscles are screaming mercy.*
> *Why I decided to do this to myself is*
> *unknown. How can there be any benefit*
> *to doing the bitter experience of lifting a*
> *weight repeatedly until your body can't*
> *lift it anymore?*

"Very good, remember last time you were here James? You explained how burnt out and stressed you were. Practicing gratitude when writing in your journal is a good idea, just being thankful, giving praise, appreciation, and compliments to aspects in life can be a benefit to your mind."

"I do remember and I am to do this whenever I get down and have another break down. You said I need to pick and choose what I find most effective when facing my demons."

"Correct, revisiting the list we compiled together is important to go back to. Spontaneity is a spice with tastes better suited for certain things. Just as a person does not put garlic salt on everything they eat, a gratitude journal may not work for all the demons encountered."

"I wish I could predict the future so my circumstances in life are more certain."

"The future is unpredictable, certainty has a paradox of the opposite being uncertain, which is on the other side of the spectrum. I guess a certain way to look at it is having the stoic mindset. A person can place certainty on what they do, respond, and think to what happens."

"That's so limited, I feel helpless, why can't the odds, the probability be more in my favor?"

"Morality is the cause of your dilemma, you will have to fix the game of life, this is cheating. Your reputation will be ruined in the eyes of others."

"Why should I care about my reputation, I don't like most people. Human interaction is too folly, too lame."

"Human behavior is far from perfect, so many mistakes, just throw most of it away as invaluable."

"Well, I should get going, thanks again Dianne," says James standing to leave while putting both arms through the straps of his back pack.

⤔

"So I face the chance of either having to wait or act now in pursuing a woman to court for marriage," says Griffin with spontaneity.

"Yes, act now Griffin," says Lara.

"If I act now, I will pursue with a vengeance, all or nothing. I will go all out and pursue them with everything I have."

"Wow, hold on," says Lara.

"Here's an example, man meets woman and woman asks man to dance with her. Man says, 'I don't dance.' Woman asks man to dance again. Man is hesitant and says, 'okay.' Man side steps and taps his feet a few times and says, 'There.' Woman says, 'That's not enough. Man must go all out and live life to the fullest and dance longer,'" says Griffin.

Lara chuckles at Griffin's example. The cold wintry air blows into the bar as the door opens for a group of people entering the busy Friday night venue. The bar is hopping, close to exceeding the fifty person maximum established by the local fire department. A neon glow of blue comes casting down onto Lara's face, a reflection off of the window she is facing towards sitting at the table.

The usual layout of the bar is that of a rectangle with restrooms in the back next to the exit. The seating on one side and the bar with rear kitchen on the other, not like the unique floor plans you see on Broadway. Above all the beer company signs hanging on the wall are a top row of TV's, flat screen and die cast car models sitting on mantles. The bar name, "Classic Car Bar" after the owner's obsession with classic cars. The seating has car seats, the napkins and salt and pepper shakers are located in glove compartments, and there is an engine block on display by the exit door. Tail and headlights make up the overhead lighting and the lower trim on the walls are made of car bumpers, however, the most appealing aspect is the wallpaper showing a picture of classic cars from the 1920's era through the 1970's.

"You see even if I tried to be moderate in this someone will pressure me to do more and I just can't resist the temptation," says Griffin.

"I got to go," says Lara.

She grabs her coat, which is hanging on the back of her chair. She is still laughing about Griffin's analogy.

"Did you know?" says Griffin slouching back in his chair relaxed.

"Know what?" says Lara.

"While walking a rope at an elevated height, there are over a thousand ways to fall off and only a hand full of ways to get across."

"Really, I did not know that. Are you sure that is right?"

"No, I'm not for sure," says Griffin with a smile on his face, "Just an interesting fact I came up with."

"Well, I don't know if that is a fact per se. More like an idea that you came up with."

"Lara, I'm going to take in as much air as I can by taking in a deep breath. Then I want you to punch me in the chest," says Griffin with a mischievous look on his face.

Griffin inhales a big breath and takes a couple more small breaths to try and fill more air into his lungs.

"I'm not going to punch you."

"Why not? I'm giving you a free shot."

"It's not happening."

He stands on his car seat, acting as if to get a big crowd's attention while holding a beer bottle as if it was a microphone.

"Can I have your attention? Can I have your attention please? Welcome to another session of the "Man Meets Woman" series. Man meets woman, man asks woman to have coffee with him. Woman has coffee with man and pours hot coffee all over man's face. Man gets third degree burns. Woman teaches man a lesson about trying to pursue woman."

"Okay, now you're embarrassing yourself Griffin."

## PITY PARTY

Walking up the stairs of the office building is fiercely fatiguing for James. The elevator is down for maintenance, which makes sense because the building seems to be older than anyone here. Doors, windows, and hallways are narrower and smaller than new buildings today.

The reception area to Trident Investing is also small with the receptionist seated at a small desk six feet away from a row of five chairs and a coffee table. James takes a seat and crosses one leg over the other, resting his left index finger over his left temple in deep thought going over possible questions he could be asked in the job interview.

The logo of Trident Investments is not a trident, it's a bow quiver drawn back with three arrows in it. James is wearing a blue suit and tie with white undershirt. His shoes are black leather to match his eye glasses and black hair. The person giving the interview is an older man in his sixties. Just by looking at him, you could tell he had experience. The experiences of many failures and fewer successes, of these few successes, one was a bigger success than them all; this success was bigger than expected and was unexpected. A run of good luck, a wind fall like no other to make up for all the previous losses, hitting the jackpot, winning the lottery, it didn't get any better than that. The interviewer wears kakis, dress shirt is white with red tie, slim body, skinny, and broad cheek bones. His side burns have greying hair. His demeanor is not calm and the tone of his voice explains that he has already had an awful confrontation today and is in the process of trying to move on from it.

Before the interview starts, a brunette woman in her thirties holding a leather binder enters and sits next to the interviewer. This will be a two person interview. The first thing she does is express her hectic morning dealing with too cool for Mom teenagers at home and employees who leave food in the fridge for longer than a week. You can tell she is a people person with likability.

"My name is Kate, James why are you interested in working at Trident Investments?"

"My skills showcase productivity multipliers to improve cost measures and efficiency," James says with a nervous stutter to his voice.

"Productivity multipliers, give me an example of how that applies to our financial products," says Kate.

"Productivity multipliers are reached at full employment or when unemployment is below five percent, this creates efficiency, takes slack out of the work, and demand has to be high for the productivity multiplier to work. Weak demand has features of slow cash flows such as weak growth, high unemployment, and no jobs or investments being made, just a full-on stagnate economy overall."

"Give me an example of a coworker conflict you've had in the past and what steps you took to resolve it."

"I had a disagreement with my previous business partner on a sales goal not being met. He was too laid back about it and waiting too long without enough initiative. I resolved the problem by being assertive in trying to get his perspective by first seeking to understand, then being understood from my perspective. Overall, I went from being passive-aggressive, to being assertive in the situation to use empathy. It's important to know where both people stand in terms of opinions."

"Why should we hire you for the position of Lead Underwriter?"

"I've been underwritten previously and know what customers are looking for when financing their business. I can relate with them, which will build trust."

⁂

Griffin and Lara sit in their living room relaxing and watching TV. The flat screen sits on a wall mounted mantel. Below, the surround sound speakers and broad band device sit in what used to be the old entertainment center. Griffin has his feet up on the foot rest of the recliner and Lara lays out completely taking up the entire couch. The walk way into the living room is in between the recliner and couch.

"I enjoy playing to lose, getting my face stomped into the ground. I lose so that other people can win. I look into the mirror and see shit, and hell, I even smell like shit. Well, if I look like shit and smell like shit, I must be shit," says Griffin. After a moment's pause, out of the blue he says. "Three plus one is five."

"No, that's wrong," says Lara with an odd look on her face.

"Three plus one is five when you use your imagination to fill in the rest. When you have nothing at all to make five for example, zero plus zero is five. This is what you would call *Alice in Wonderland* imagination. An entire world made up, which is an example of poverty creating something totally new out of nothing."

"Let's change the subject. Oh, tell me another episode of 'Man Meets Woman'!"

"Here's an episode of 'Man Meets Woman'. Man meets woman and a month later woman becomes pregnant with man's baby. Man's mother is furious with the social status of the pregnant woman and has a bad vibe about her. Man's father feels the same way and says nothing. Man's father forever holds his peace. Man's father says openly in front of man and woman, 'This is a good thing with the addition of a new child. Thinking otherwise will only hurt the people involved.'"

"You forget to explain what the man sees when meeting the women for the first time in detail. He sees the woman's facial expression of seduction; with those Google eyes…it can move mountains. A woman's seductive look has great power and provides the man joy. It makes the man feel he has the world by the ass and want to climb the highest mountain. Since the seductive woman is priceless for the man, the woman should make sure to use this power responsibly. Henceforth, the look of a woman's seduction can be a form of deception and trickery. She is innocent if looking seductive to another man, if not seeing anybody. She is guilty if seductively gazing at a man and seeing someone else," says Lara becoming engaged in the storytelling activity.

"Perhaps, the man went up to the woman and asks her on a date for his self interests and he wants her to be in his life. Or is it he wants to be in her life, to give her a fulfilling life. A woman asks a man to go on a date so she can be a part of his life, so she can care for him. Which reason is more innocent? Wanting the other person to be in your life or wanting to be in their life to provide and care for them? Giving is better than taking and being under obligation right? Instead of looking in terms of their life and my life, look at both lives together as whole. Therefore, a man asks a woman on a date to create a fulfilling life. A woman asks a man to a date to create a better life. Interesting, man goes to confront a woman and try to get into her life. Man has to let her know how much she means to him. Man walks over to the woman seated three tables away, the woman asks, 'Can I help you?' 'I'm good, but I smell fear. I can smell fear when it's present. This fear in not from the person I'm looking at,' says the man. The woman looks around and notices there is no one else around and the person he is looking at is her. 'This fear I smell is from my own worst enemy, my own worst enemy is me,' says the man. 'Sounds like a personal problem. I'm interested in finding out more about this fear and the person behind it,' says the woman. 'Have you ever seen a woman make a fool of herself? I have seen one very, very recently. Yes, recently like five seconds ago recently,' says man. The woman smiles, bites her lower lip and looks down at the table she's sitting at."

⁂

"Let's get everyone together and shame you," says Stacy with sarcasm.

James sits in his apartment with his girlfriend making chili by mixing canned tomatoes, beans, chili mix, and ground beef. A stressed out week at work and James is having the burnout occur again.

"Yes, then I can take the fall, then I will become a martyr. I'm little, petite, and puny. I'm not a man. I'm a boy, this will fuel my low self-esteem and suppress my ego," says James matching Stacy's sarcasm.

"You're a pathetic man, a douche bag, an egotistical asshole, a dick head, and a womanizer," Stacy responds.

"You're a dumb cunt. Hey, you call me by my genitals, I'll call you by yours, seems fair."

"We need to take care of ourselves and right now we're failing," says Stacy trying to switch the subject. She recognizes this is not a joke anymore, comedy has turned into tragedy.

"Marriage is just a legal form of prostitution. Really, love is about the money, then divorce happens and extortion occurs. Divorce lawyers get a third of my net worth, you get a third, maybe, just maybe, I'll get a third, unless you totally clean me out," says James taking the conversation personally.

"Oh, let's just throw a big pity party for you!"

"Pity, I love it. I love feeling sorry for myself."

"Put a filter on both of our mouths. Why can't you just compromise with me? Who cares, go on, just continue and get it out."

"It's the price of liberty, individualism, and the highest price-your American dream. I'm not willing to pay the price; therefore, I should not have it."

"The money, huh? The love of money is the root of all evil you know."

"Yes, the money is what is important. In terms of evil, I'm already in hell. I want the money because of what it represents. It represents safety. Regarding compromise, I have paid for necessities. I've tried to meet you half way, we use the method of my money, our money, and your money, all divided equally, remember?"

"Yes, I remember, we agreed to provide for each other. You want to open up a beauty boutique and I want to be a successful entrepreneur, this all takes money."

"Why do you like pity, shame, and regret? Why are you so hard on yourself?"

"I lack confidence. Rather than wanting to brag about myself, I want to put my troubles onto others in order to get their attention. The attention is other people feeling sorry for me."

"So, you're saying you're being a damsel in distress. Well, I don't like your show of pity, stop it! Stop bringing out craziness."

"I will try. I guess I'm desiring to bring everyone down to my level of hardship, if I can endure more pain, suffering, and hardship than anyone, I will last longer than everyone else because I'm stronger. I can endure more. If I can't beat other people at their game, I'll beat them by having to play my game."

"I do not want to play your game of self-pity."

"I know because of individualism, liberty, choice theory, and democracy right?"

"That and I no longer want to hear your ranting. God, that class was such a long time ago, do you remember?"

"I'm a coward; I'm willing to accept failure and a loss."

"No, you're not a coward. Cowards run away from their problems. You don't run away, you stick to problems until they are solved."

"You have to know when to quit. It's important for a person not to think costs previously made go in vain. Previous costs cannot be made up, they are a loss and putting more money, time, and effort is not going to make up for prior losses."

Stacy turns off the voice recorder on the kitchen counter recording the conversation. James notices this and makes direct eye contact with his girlfriend.

"I want you to take this recording to your next Psychiatrist meeting to let her listen. I want her to hear with what I am dealing with," says Stacy with a caring tone in her voice.

## RESOLVE

At a roadside diner in Baltimore, James and Griffin meet just to catch up on old times. The waitresses are serving coffee, the cooks are in the back flipping omelets and pancakes, and the early morning customers are talking about the latest rumors in the city. Rumors of what sports teams will do in the off season, wins and losses during the season, election politics, the military academy bringing in another group of recruits to Baltimore Harbor, and other top headlines making the news.

The tension from the failed business is still dividing James and Griffin. If anybody still holds a grudge it's James, Griffin doesn't take things personally. It's just part of doing business. James reads the news on his smart phone and Griffin is busy text messaging Lara, "XOXOXO".

"Lover Boy, so what do you have planned now?" asks James.

"James, you've come a long way from sitting in a coffee shop with two grand in your name. Just look at what you have built, the castle of the world is in the palm of your hand," says Griffin ignoring the question and refusing to make the conversation about him.

"Yes, while I was working for two decades into the future. You were living for today. Why couldn't either of us have a more balanced approach to the way we did things?" asks James.

"Seek meekness or seek humbleness, perhaps, there is no such thing as balance when seeking your best performance. The efforts needed to achieve equilibrium and balance takes away from one's full capability," says Griffin.

"I challenge you one last time to a competition of your choice."

"Oh, wrong choice that would give me home field advantage James."

"I have an equal chance of winning no matter the game."

"What is at stake?"

"Anything you want, I have nothing to lose. I'm already naked and against all the odds. You know me, I know no other way of doing it,"

"Yes, you've always been all in."

"The game, Name the Price. Do you still remember how to play?"

"Yes, each player predicts tomorrows closing commodity prices in the stock market. The person closest to the seven commodity prices of gold, oil, beef, corn, ten-year bond note, iron ore, and steel will win the game. The person having the most incorrect price estimate will pay the price by handing over ten percent of their estate value."

"That's not fair, how are we to know how much a person has in their estate?"

"Try to look at this as bragging rights to getting the best of a long-time friendly competition."

"It's a Woomon, see," says Griffin pointing in the direction of a young woman walking their way. The lady has black hair, red and white waitress dress, a good luck charm bracelet dangles loosely from her left wrist, and she carries a note pad to take menu orders. She walks towards their table.

"Are you talking about a Pokémon or something?" asks James.

"No, a woomon, it's a woomon."

"Hi, my name is Mary. Are you ready to order?" asks Mary the waitress.

"Mary, I want to talk to your High Commander," says Griffin.

"You mean my supervisor, my boss?" asks Mary.

"Your high commander, fearless leader, you know your dictator."

"Yep, he's on vacation, but I can give you the contact to his aristocrat executive, bourgeoisie friends, and his master chief relatives."

"Ha ha! I see what you are trying to do. You're copying me. Well, Minion Mary I will see to it your High Commander reprimands you for that."

"What lesson will I learn?" asks Mary.

"I'm just joking, relax you're not in trouble," says Griffin

"Griffin, be polite, that is no way to treat her. Sorry, you will have to excuse my friend, I don't know what is wrong with him," says James.

"I do have problems," says Griffin circling his index finger by his temple to indicate he is crazy. "I'm here, but I'm not here. I've lost my grip on reality. I was here, but now I'm there, and now I'm not here anymore."

"Yes, ready to order now please, thank you," says James looking to allow Mary to get back to work.

✒

At James's next Psychiatrist session with Dianne, he plays the recording of his conversation of pity and shame with Stacy. Again, Newton's Cradle swings back and forth and the overcast sky makes the office darker with deep shadows being cast to the floor by the furniture and book cases. One surprise is recognizing a solved Rubik's Cube sitting on her desk next to her notepad, which wasn't there last time. The voice recording ends and Dianne continues to write on her notepad during a few minutes of silence. James turns the voice recorder off.

"We have a lot of information to look at today, this voice recording, and two journal entries. Now let's go over the journal entries, shall we? Read it out loud James," suggests Dianne.

James reads:

> *The body resumes, senses return, and looking over at my alarm clock, it reads 5:12. Gazing out my bedroom window with my half closed sleepy eyes, there is a little daylight showing. You can tell the sun will rise soon. Now is the time when an ambitious duty comes to mind. The dilemma is whether to start the day now or rest for eight minutes waiting for my alarm clock to go off.*
>
> *I think to myself heck with it, the sooner it starts the sooner it ends.*

*Standing up out of bed, blood fills my sleepy limbs, it all starts now. My body is slow from sleeping. The testing's and trials of the day ahead. The discomfort, which is not suffering, but only I think it is suffering because it is one of the most difficult parts of my day. Sometimes all it takes is to show up and the workout will take care of itself. Today, I'm thinking how I will get through the workout when I'm already this tired.*

*Heading to the kitchen, I grab my water bottle to fill it up with tap water at the sink. Upon shutting the faucet off, the water continues to drip slowly, drip by drip. Just as day by day I continue to workout at the gym. I walk out the door with my gym bag. First, I shuffle through my music selection of Rock n Roll on my IPod player, which is low on batteries because I forgot to charge it again, happens all the time. Second, I stretch to try and loosen up and condition every muscle for a full body workout. Third, the best series of exercises comes to mind, off the top of my head. When working out, you have to be able to think on the fly to incorporate a full body workout. After taking a quick swig of water, the intimidating workout is a challenging task requiring hard work to complete. The motivation required to embark on such a task requires a personalized intrinsic reason to do so.*

*Doing super sets where a person performs two exercises, one right after another without a break. Up to a minute break is allowed before conducting the next set. Three of these sets are done. The first exercises are Goblin Squats and Military Press. Squats have my legs tired on the last rep due to my blood not being able to keep up with my stored muscles demands. The last set of the Military press is going to be a difficult task. While drinking from the water bottle, I say, 'Finish It. Just do it as Nike ads say.' At the sixth rep of the Military Press my shoulders are already burning, at eight reps the barbell almost cannot be lifted, and at ten reps requires everything I have left to complete. This last rep takes about five seconds to do.*

*Deadlifts, bench press, and sit-ups are next, with the Deadlifts taking the most amount of energy out of me. I take a quick break with a drink of water. Some exercises are more enjoyable to do for vanity's sake than others, depending on personal preference. The women at the gym wear tight clothing to show off their bodies, the men show off their chest and arms. Whether looking at form in front of the mirror, spotting someone, or having a dazed stare from someone across the gym, there is definitely a mind complex regarding appearance going on at gyms today.*

*The end of the workout has the level of tiredness being even greater. My mind is telling me to quit, but the heart; the ego inside of me is knocking at the door saying, 'Do not give in. You will persevere.' Just like in the Foo Fighters song playing on the IPod, "Best of You" you are either born to resist or be abused. You see, it's like a game between a person and adversity. Pushing yourself takes a toll. The mind wants fast changes; this only happens occasionally and mental toughness is essential to keep going.*

*After the last rep of my third set, the dumbbell drops to the floor making a loud noise for everyone in the gym to hear. This is bad gym etiquette; I've been talk to before by the staff about my bad gym etiquette. It slipped okay; my arms feel lifeless and might fall off their sockets. About a half a minute later guilt sets in, 'Should I do more? I shouldn't over do it.'*

*Ending with some simple stretching exercises to loosen muscles up and circulate blood flow to carry off waste products from my muscles. By now, my IPod is getting to the end of the playlist. The thought of accomplishment at this point is rewarding. I walk out of the entrance to the gym. The body and mind are relaxed, totally spent, confident, and feeling as if the weight of the world can be put back onto my shoulders.*

"The second journal entry reads as follows," says James turning the page in his journal to continue reading to Dianne.

*In the book of Job, the prime example is shown about the comeback story. Some people lose everything at some point in their life and lose confidence in their ability. They are beaten to a whim with a morsel of strength left to pursue their aspirations. The people able to turn outcomes around have given more to their efforts than expected. They started a project and had it turn into a mess of problems in a grand mass. Looking at the grand mass a person see's nothing but struggles, shame from others and a price to pay beyond imagine. To devote yourself to such an idea, ideal, cause, or ethical dilemma is a great way to go to work on something beyond one's self. Better yet, the grand mass being spoken of ends up helping others to create unexpected results that no one could have predicted. In the end, pursuit of self interests can turn out to benefit others, and the price of this is going to require others to pay in order for this to happen. The key to this is having delayed gratification and delayed rewards.*

"In comparison between the two journal entries, there is a common theme of enduring difficulty and delayed rewards afterwards. What are those celebrations you speak of?" Asks Dianne.

"I will eat some comfort food or just take an entire day off, a guilty pleasure," says James with a smirk on his face.

"If only your high aspirations and goals could have been followed up with celebration, the enjoyment of your own work in your journal entries to complete the entire process. You see, the difficulty is experienced, but not the reward. Next time I want you to journal about both. If you are not explaining both in your journal you're not experiencing both. Even if you don't reward yourself each day, still describe the day off of doing nothing or the delicious comfort food."

"I will do that next time."

"I think you get burnt out James, so you need a frequent reward program too. Emotional intelligence is the new term today to describe an individual's ability to recognize emotions with empathy. This is intelligence recognizes with awareness the emotions of yourself and others. I think doing this will help with personal/professional relationships and relationship you have with the day to day difficulties described in your journal. Now, you need to respect Stacy and not call her vulgar names, even if you are joking. If I were you, I would apologize and not put your problems onto her."

"Thank you Dianne, I will do that. I should get going now," says James leaving the office with his journal in hand.

# SALES DRIVE

Griffin's house is a three bedroom two bath, two story house with a detached garage to reduce taxes. The outside solar panels on the roof create a tax deduction every year and extra electricity can be sold as credit to the electric company. Inside the house, Lara and him are making Teriyaki Chicken in the oven. She gets the brown sugar, soy sauce, and Teriyaki sauce together while he gets the chicken breasts ready to marinate. The oven is a new Honeywell oven with the timer set for twenty-five minutes.

In the meantime, while they wait, the couple goes to the living room area and sits together on the couch. Above the couch are a shoulder mount of a bull caribou and a mount of a king salmon fish, both taken in Alaska. With white shoulders and a brown head, the caribou has C-shaped antlers. The king salmon has a bright red underbelly and big head. The fish and caribou mounts are the same size. Lara has some décor of her own with a wreath hanging on the wall made from willow branches acorns and flower pedals. Both the kitchen and dining room have candles. The living room has a sectional couch made of black leather and family photos hang on the wall. The lights in the living and dining rooms are on the walls so the walls themselves have no shadows. All shadows are cast down onto the floor.

As Griffin and Lara sit on the couch holding hands, they explain their dreams that are yet to be fulfilled. Lara wants a raised garden next to her She-Shed, and outdoor pool with a deck and a landscaped water fall. Griffin wants to add an addition to the house with a back porch to relax in and a game room for his gambling habits.

"I'm not a bad man, I'm just not a good man," says Griffin.

"Be careful for Lady Liberty, she bites," says Lara.

"Why did you do that? Why did you say that?" A pause occurs, at least thirty seconds long. He just continues to stare at the wall, as if day dreaming. "Sometimes when God doesn't answer your prayers or questions, does God answer you every time? It's like that. Just because I'm not responding to you does not mean I'm not listening," says Griffin trying to explain his selective hearing. "I like my seclusion, that way I do not get distracted with branching out the conversation into a different direction, a different train of thought."

"Is that really a bad thing? You also have the ability to branch out the topic to your intended direction in a tit for tat strategy."

"Are there more options than that? I can choose to not participate in your topic of conversation, start with a different topic, or match your topic of conversation with further information being given."

"Why do you like seclusion? Don't you like to spend time with me?"

"Every time I'm with you I feel like I'm being judged for wrong doing and being lectured by your father."

"My father, why?"

"If I make one mistake and he hears about it. If I break your heart or don't buy into your American Dream, he'll break my nose and my fingers. I don't want to pay for your American Dream. It's too expensive."

"I think you're making a big deal out of what my dreams are. Your anxiety and habit of being too hard on yourself is self-defeating you. It's a double edged sword."

"The police I'm afraid of also. If we fight and I physically or verbally abuse you, you will call the police and they will come and take me away."

"Yep, you're right; I'm not going to deal with that shit."

"Distractions make it so I cannot get anything done. Too many distractions and I cannot focus on my work."

"You need to simplify and cut out the excess in order to fine tune and edit for perfection."

"I work with focus up to forty minutes at a time. My mind gets tired. I see a spectrum of distractions on one end and burnt out focus on the other."

"It could also be a bell curve or peak and trough on a graph."

"Yes, the variables would have to be focus, distractions, and productivity. What do you know? Three variables would make a curved line on a graph."

"Where focus and productivity are positively correlated. Distractions and focus/productivity are negatively correlated."

"Wow, this is a weird topic to talk about. I think we've lost our grip on reality."

"No, it's all you, you're the delusional one. I'm the normal one."

"No, no, no, you're the crazy one."

"Why are you using all your time to help someone else, when you can use that time to focus on improving yourself."

"Yeah, if I don't get my work done what would happen? I would fail right."

"You're not going to be able to keep up with the work. It's not sustainable; you're going to piss a lot of people off."

"I've upset many people in my life. We live in a limited world, that world is small with limited opportunity. Get rid of the ceiling and walls to create unlimited potential, the sky is the limit. You need to realize barriers of the mind can make you an expert sitting in a cubicle. Have a mindset of a new individual being naïve. That is how you'll discover something unique."

"Unlimited amount of earnings, I will earn more money."

"Yep, you will earn a paycheck," she looks with a hideous glare.

"Not the look, anything but the look, HHHAAA!!!" says Griffin with sarcasm. He sits down and looks up to her standing in front of him. Holding her hand in his, he gives her forehand a soft kiss and looks up into her eyes. "You're so beautiful, you're body has so many curves. Everywhere on your body there is a cheek for me to kiss."

Lara smiles, sits next to Griffin on the couch and throws her arms around him to embrace each other with a lovely kiss.

෧

The hotel is a long rectangular building with the convention center next to it. Looking as if a cereal box is next to a shoe box on the kitchen counter, the building has modern architecture design with tan stucco on the outside. A circle drive-up is in front of the hotel with three flags flapping furiously in the wind. The roof of the hotel entrance casts a dark shadow from the sun, which is now behind the building. There are two shadows with the shadow of the hotel entrance being darker than the shadow cast by the building. Inside Hank Hawk is that shadow, he sits in his dark room, on the top floor, like a king in his castle.

"It's a form of equity; it's something that no one else has. It differentiates me from everyone else. This country has people who think like cowboys, their all way too conservative. Ultra conservative, I like to say, not willing to take risks," says Hank Hawk.

"Or it's just being patient, waiting for the right opportunity," says Francis, one of Hank's associates.

Hank Hawk is upset and yells with pride, "I'm a rock star. I have the money, I do the drugs, get all the pretty women!"

"Not me, I like to think of myself as a Puritan, working hard and having very few thrills in life. One question Mr. Hawk, why do you take everyone for a run?"

"Let me tell you a story, when I was young my father would try and trick me into thinking I was getting a good deal. Later in life is when I realized how it was a bad deal. My father was in debt, he owed everyone money and played the game for the short-term. He would rob Peter to pay Paul; it was a never ending racket, back and forth. Just like the story of the scorpion and the frog, I was the frog getting stung by the older people, the scorpions. Today, I'm the scorpion, now it's my turn to sting."

"Shouldn't you be stinging the older generation who did that to you? Your grudge is with them not me."

"I'm done getting back at what was done to me. It's not just about the seniors picking on the youngsters. It's within every person as a characteristic of human behavior and this will go on forever. Its nature, I did get my revenge and in the process of taking my revenge out on others it became easier. This is why I continue to do it, I'm obsessed and it's easy. You're getting all emotional, right vs. wrong, ethics and morality, my own father would do this to me. What makes you think I would do the right thing no matter the cost?"

&#8450;

James steps into the five storied Trident Investments office building in a professional attire black business suit, red tie. The bright lighting shines off of his forehead and copper covered walls. The floor is white linoleum tile and the window lighting mainly comes from the atrium entrance. James walks past the main lobby reception desk to the stairwell where he will climb to the third floor. Upon reaching the third floor, the hallways make the form of a rectangular figure eight. Offices and meeting rooms make up the third floor of the building.

First, James has an 8:30 meeting with Trident Investments CEO, Financial Analyst, Accountants, and Shareholders'. In the meeting, James is very nervous looking over the future forecasts the Financial Analyst is presenting.

"Profit margins are going to be down twenty percent next quarter? Well, what are we going to do about it?" asks CEO Tim Sherling.

The meeting room and everyone in it goes silent. The air conditioning starts from the ventilation shaft and begins to make a humming sound. James decides to give input into the situation.

"Increasing profit margins next quarter by charging buyers higher fees and have the accountant look at tax reduction possibilities; get more customers in this low business cycle we're in. Oh, and have outstanding receivables pay up within a thirty-five day period rather than a sixty day period. If no payment is made on their annual fees in thirty-five days, let's let them know how we do business," says James spinning his pen sideways on the glass table top.

"This is a low cycle we're seeing, I agree with that. What James says makes sense, but might be too drastic of a change. Sometimes the best approach to problem solving is applying patience, grace, and being calm. To dramatize and agitate the problem further will blow this out of proportion," says Shelly the Financial Analyst in her mid-thirties, wearing a purple blouse.

"I agree with Shelly, if we recognize the problem coming from the market and not necessarily the business. Then, the problem will solve itself during the market upswing," says a shareholder, David Spearman.

"We need to adapt to the market and be proactive. Tim just asked everyone what we are going to do about the profit margin problem we face in the upcoming months. Doing nothing is not doing anything," says James.

CEO Tim Sherling smiles at James's comment. He massage's his temples with both index fingers. The bottom jaw shakes nervously as he opens his mouth to speak his mind, "I like the idea of more marketing for new investors, getting a higher percentage of outstanding receivables back, and selling the Hart Lakeshore Association to a smaller real estate investment trust."

"How was your day at work honey?" asks Stacy sitting on the couch, reading the latest issue of *Reader's Digest*.

"Tough, getting tougher by the day," James responds taking his shoes off at the front door.

"You are going crazier and crazier by the day."

"No, I'm not, that's foolish."

"Yes, your crazy has been evolving, when you bring out crazy, it has changed, you've been adding more things to it. More complexes, more personalities just like a puppet master with multiple puppets, your crazy has a crazy within crazy, that's an interesting dynamic."

"Or I could be ranting to myself. Look Dianne said to try emotional intelligence and journaling about rewards. I'm also sorry for what I said to you last week."

"You have my forgiveness. Are you getting enough sleep at night? You know sleep deprivation can ruin your attitude and ability to handle stress."

"Yeah, I can probably improve in that department. I work for an evil dictator, every action I do at work is motivated by fear of her evil tactics."

"Watch out, she might bite."

"I think she is sadistic, she gets satisfaction from watching other people suffer."

"Is it your birthday today?"

"Yeah, I don't celebrate birthdays. It's an unspoken rule in my family, you see when I was growing up my dad put all of his money into the mortgage payment and I grew up in a house with nothing in it. He was always so proud of my mother for driving fifteen year old beater cars."

"Your dad must have been cheap. You're not a cheapskate are you?"

"Don't judge him, don't judge me. My dad sacrificed a lot to get what he has."

"Yeah, nobody makes any money off of him because he is cheap."

"In terms of pride, everyone there at work thinks they're the most important person in the building, their proud of their pride, they have a God complex. Talk about being anal, they have a serious competition going on inside psychologically."

"That usually doesn't end well, end for the better anyway," says Stacy going back to reading her magazine.

# CONVERTIBLE BONDS

With sombreros hanging on the wall and Mexican music playing softly on the speakers, the Mexican Restaurant, Quesadilla Grande is hopping busy this evening. The main chef has an obsession for cheese. The windows and doorways have the shape of a half circle with brown stucco walls. Mexican pottery sits on mantles, saddle blankets are draped under banjo guitars, and the red and white waitress dresses match the red and white curtains of the windows. The red table cloth matches the curtain also, which makes the color red subconsciously represent the main attraction of the service waitresses, the beautiful view from the windows, and the great food.

Lara sits across the table from Griffin. Spending the evening wining and dining on margaritas and enchiladas are one of Lara's favorite treats. Her father was Mexican, coming to America to work the seasonal potato harvest in the summer and switching to a dairy farm in the winter months. Lara wears her hair down, finely combed to reach her shoulders. She has on a white blouse and black skirt to match her black high heels, the lip stick, mascara, and earrings are violet with black eye liner.

Griffin is in a somber mood this evening after a hectic week at the firm. His dark orange turtle neck sweater, tan kakis, and brown leather shoes match the in-season fall colors. The big oak tree seen outside the entrance window has orange leaves falling to the ground after the first of many seasonal frosts. Griffin has a big lot of worries on his mind about his business. For the evening, he's trying get a buzz from the third Corona beer he is drinking. Relaxing his insecurities of risk, he tries to let go of his worries, trying to make Monday's payroll deadline and the company's loan payments by the end of the week. The buzz of being drunk creates a temporary reset for him to move on from the previous week and start a new one.

"I love Mexican food," says Lara looking through her menu to order.

"I know, that's why I brought you here. Oh, just a reminder you are stunningly beautiful tonight," says James making eye contact with Lara with a surprise look on his face.

"Thanks, that's so sweet Griff."

After a thirty second pause, the many thoughts going through Lara's minds comes to an abrupt conclusive response. "Okay, what are you up to Griffin?"

"I want it to be a surprise. Well okay," Griffin raises his right arm in the air and snaps his fingers. Three Mexican banjo players quickly walk over to their table and play a Mexican lullaby song. Griffin digs in his pocket, gets down on one knee, and looks up into Lara's brown eyes. "Lara, will you marry me?" asks Griffin with the happiest face he could make.

Lara doesn't answer until fifteen seconds later. "Yes…yes, yes, I will marry you."

The Mexican banjo switch to a faster beat fiesta song. Griffin and Lara kiss and hug.

"Great, let's order some desert!" says Griffin.

✐

Sitting at home in his study, James is reading a crime thriller novel with a twist at the end. The protagonist and antagonist meet at the end for a final confrontation. When the antagonist reveals his real identity, he does not answer for his crime because he is a person with high reputation in the community. Instead, there is cover up in order to keep the true identity a secret and giving the figure a pen name. The person who takes the fall for the antagonist's crime is not a real person.

Having a highly reputable good guy turn bad would ruin the people's self-esteem.

Books half read pile up on the edges of his desk, three, five, or six books stacked flat on top of each other in columns. The cluttered and disorganized desk has little working space. The silence in the room is so quiet you can hear voices in the house talking from downstairs. A tapping from the furnace can be heard from the air duct, this is what it does when powering down.

James is wearing his favorite comfortable sweat pants, and a fleece pullover. This allows him to pay attention and focus more energy towards his train of thought, the voice inside his head, his creative hermit. No distractions, just all energy being reserved for the tasks of studying, reading, and writing. His elbows are sore from resting them on his desk while studying for a long time. Many lessons, skills, and adventures have been experienced in this room, many of them have been forgotten, some have stuck in his memory, and few have been put to good use. The same can be said of the projects started, few were ever finished to the end and one was only successful. The thesis paper for his Master's in Business degree. The intensified focus it took to achieve a flow state was hard work when writing the thesis. James remembered a certain point during the writing process that obtained peak creativity, an aha moment, an epiphany. This point is when all gears were moving in synchronization, all focus was concentrating on the task at hand, he was sitting in his study, but his mind wasn't there at all. Being awarded the Business Model Projections and Restructuring Award for the study of business model changes in probability loan defaults and bankruptcy. The award is framed next to his Master's degree from Wharton's Business School.

"I have so much that I do not know what to do with it all. I'm not able to use all the things I have. I cannot use my possessions wisely. My possessions own me, they sit there and mock me, I'm overwhelmed with not being able to use any of them enough. I buy them only to use them once and go on to never using them again. I know the more I take in possessions, the more I take things for granted," says James talking Stacy.

"So much of the world is unspoken communication. People choose not to express themselves because they want to keep a secret, do not want to be seen as radical in their views so they have a filter over their mouth, or they do not recognize a need to express. This passion has made you work harder without any results to show for it, with no results to speak of you've created a snare. You're a workaholic becoming obsessed with your work. You lose track of time, forgetting to pick up the dry cleaners and the kids from school. You work yourself to the bone, look at you, you're rail thin," says Stacy.

"I'm perfecting and mastering my craft. You don't understand, my work transforms me into an alternative reality. I have done everything I could have ever imagined, and so I have done everything I could have ever imagined... And some."

"Turn this difficulty into an enjoyable activity."

"What are you talking about? Work isn't supposed to be fun."

"You get what you ask for, that and everything that goes along with it. You're worried about something that may or may not happen two years from now? Don't plan for something that might happen. If it happens, it happens. We'll deal with it when it does or doesn't happen. Right now, you're overestimating costs and threats," says Stacy with a pause to reflect on what she has yet to say. "Communication occurs in a circle, what starts with you will eventually come back to you. Usually first the secret is revealed. Second, the informant is revealed."

"I'm thinking about going to an entrepreneurial seminar, two hundred dollars for the weekend."

"Yeah, sounds good because free advice is worthless. Worthless I tell you, worthless!"

"Laughter and self-doubt killed my American Dream. That's right the critics and doubters took my dreams away."

"You need to maintain a calm demeanor, emotional intelligence remember."

~

The luxury yacht is white, three floors high, and fifty yards long. A helicopter pad at the rear and a pool in the front, the yacht is named, *Memo Mori* to signify nothing lasts forever. The waves on the Atlantic Ocean coastal waters are fierce today. The white caps steadily push and splash against the hull. Servants dressed in grey pullovers and grey pants ready the wine, whiskey, and champagne. Wine and shot glasses are placed onto the prepared serving trays. The heavy hitting customer is on the front of his yacht smoking a cigarette. The cold breeze descends down from the northwest, which the yacht is traveling into. The customer has a grey beard and wears a white sea captain's hat with black brim, and a white uniform to match. The inbound helicopter can be heard overhead, circles the yacht once and slowly descends to gently land at the rear of the yacht's landing zone. Griffin exits the aircraft and carries a briefcase to the deck next to the landing zone. A servant greets Griffin and takes him below deck. Meeting the customer with an introduction.

"Mr. Winthrop, nice to meet you sir," says Griffin shaking the captain's hand.

"Nice to meet you as well."

"I was on my way to the airport this morning and couldn't stop wondering about my inability to swim and fear of the water. It's either sink or swim. I'm sure I'll find a way to keep my head above water."

A long silence, Mr. Winthrop stares into Griffin's eyes stone faced, expressionless, and never blinking.

"I'm laughing on the inside, perhaps I should have went to New York Harbor to be closer to land," Mr. Winthrop says before breaking out in laughter. "Sorry, I couldn't hold it in."

"Mr. Winthrop, the reason why I'm here is to get additional capital for my business. Hank Hawk is a partner of yours and he referred me to you in order to make a deal."

Pushing his glasses higher up on the bridge of his nose Mr. Winthrop responds with charisma. "Yes, the financing involves convertible bonds, which I can have underwritten for a nine percent cut."

"Yes, Hank told me he wanted nine percent."

"Don't get me wrong, I'm not Hank Hawk Okay? I'm Mr. Winthrop."

"Yes, Mr. Winthrop sir."

"These are corporate convertible bonds totaling 1.2 million dollars."

"1.2 million!" says Griffin with surprise at his unexpected fortunate business prospects.

"You need some capital to increase that equity, now what do you say?" says Mr. Winthrop lighting a cigarette.

"Yes, I would like to read the terms of the finance first."

"Here you be," says Mr. Winthrop pointing to his server holding a binder of documents to sign. The server hands the binder to Griffin, who starts skimming through the pages.

At the conclusion of his speed reading, Griffin signs the documents and has the money wired to business account in three days. Griffin stays the night on the yacht and has the time of his life; the party, the after party, and the withdrawal are all exceedingly too much to ask for.

✐

Mrs. Johnson is a famous woman, who became well aware of supply and demand as a merchant retailer. She has sold everything that people would pay for. She learned from her college professor that the richest people to come out of the California Gold Rush were the owners of the hardware stores, not the gold miners themselves. She took this paradox to the extreme and has done very well for herself. The circle drive at her mansion has a bronze statue of what looks to be cupid shooting an arrow at a heart. The vast lawn has endless hedge rows spanning three acres. The roman architecture of the mansion's front door has columns; the inside of the mansion had medieval gothic architecture with Victorian lights.

"You know the game Monopoly right?" asks Mrs. Johnson.

"Yeah, the children's game," says James.

"If a player owns all of a group of properties they get to make more money. If a merchant owns more of a product, commodity, or resource than anyone else they can make more money."

Behind Mrs. Johnson's mansion there is a horse stable, one acre pasture, and an indoor riding arena. A row of fully grown oak trees surround the stable and pasture, the leaves are shaded bright and dark orange depending on where the fall frost hit most.

"You have show horses?"

"I do Dressage, which is training a horse to perform a pre-determined series of movements." She points to a picture on the wall of her riding a horse of a disciplined demeanor with head perpendicular to the ground and feet chopping up and down like pistons in an engine.

"What kinds of horses do the Dressage training?"

"That one is a Friesian; I also have an Andalusian horse, one of the best breeds in the business."

"Speaking of business, shall we discuss business with Trident Investments?"

"Yes, Trident just made a new issue of bonds at five percent interest every six months."

"How much bonds are available?"

"Close to a billion dollars total."

"What is the total market cap of the company? What type of bond is it?"

"One and a half billion dollars market cap. The bond is a convertible bond with a debt obligation kicker included."

"One and a half billion plus the new bonds being issued."

"Correct."

"I'll take them all, as soon as possible."

"Take them all?" James can't believe what is happening with a surprise look on his face.

"Here is the number to my CPA; he'll take care of everything. Now, I must be on my way. I have Dressage training scheduled in half an hour. Bye now," says Mrs. Johnson walking towards the corridors for a change of clothes.

James is ecstatic; this one big buyer can provide more business than the entire market combined. Driving back to the office, he looks into the rearview mirror to see that he's blushing red in the face. At the office, he loosens his neck tie and pulls out his smart phone to call the CPA on the business card, Mr. Winthrop.

"Hi, Mr. Winthrop here."

"Yes, Mr. Winthrop, this is James, Mrs. Johnson told me to give you a call."

"Yes, Ellen just called earlier; I got some more money for you kid. I'm a real sucker for convertible bonds. I specifically like security sweeteners. Now, I'm also a sucker for the ladies as I can't decide which one to give my attention to at any given moment, what a cluster fuck. It's like I'm chasing after two rabbits at once, impossible right."

"Yes impossible, the thrill of the chase I might add."

"Look kid, have Trident Investments underwrite some convertible bonds with a security sweetener. When that happens, I'm in for three million, done deal."

"Great, that sounds terrific."

"Call me when things are ready at this number."

"Gee, thank you for your business Mr. Winthrop."

"I believe in your business relations, it's who you know, your relationship to others. Got to go, bye now," says Mr. Winthrop ending the call.

## SIX MONTHS LATER

"How could you do this to me?" asks James.

"Yep, your position is being terminated. Look, things are different with new ownership of Trident Investments. Ellen Johnson took ownership by converting bonds into stock, now she's a majority owner in the business. She doesn't want sales reps, she wants kiosks and online banking, the way of the future," says Rick, Manager of Trident Financial.

"Automated banking lacks personalized service, there is no better way to sell Trident's financial products than by having sales reps trying to achieve sales goals, pushing sales will always outperform pulling sales. There are some things that numbers can't measure, like intangibles and heart."

"Sorry James, those underwritten bonds you created with Ellen came back to get you later. If you would have never done it, she would have never converted her bonds into shares to become majority share owner in the business."

⬟

James and Griffin sit on a bench along a bike path by the river in Baltimore. The summer morning is humid with dew coating everything wet from the night before. Early summer temperature swings make condensation friendly to plants eager to drink in the moisture. People walk their dogs and joggers run by on the bike path, doing what their made to do, which is move.

The sunrise shines a glare on the water caps as the current moves along at a slow pace. It's a Monday morning and every worker is heading to work either loving or hating their job serving others. They answer to others, maybe their boss, a coworker, or a customer. They also answer to themselves, giving themselves pep talks, ranting on and on, filling their head with self-doubt or self-confidence.

"I proposed to Lara the other day, she said yes!" says Griffin with enthusiasm.

"I'm married too, married to my job," says James feeling down and bummed out.

"You don't have a job James."

"Yeah, thanks for reminding me. Well you'll be putting up the good fight now."

"What fight?" asks Griffin.

"The fight between a Protestant work ethic and living life, having 'experiences'," says James over emphasizing the word "experiences".

"Come on, grow up James."

"When I was younger, I thought I was better than everyone else. I lost my lost my swagger now. I'm not better than everyone else. I'm just an ordinary person. Am I the patsy here or am I the person not leveraging other people's efforts for my own personal gain?"

"You are working for other people, serving others; you are leverage to the boss. You are the patsy. The boss is making more money off your work than the amount of money you earn."

"Material possessions come and go, just like people come and go, everything doesn't last forever."

"I love money, even if loving money is a bad thing. Capitalism creates extraordinary possibilities, unlimited earning potential, and that's the truth. I want the truth even if it hurts me. Are we the patsy? Sure we are; we create value as human capital."

"How is business going for you?" asks James.

"Just got done underwriting 1.2 million dollars in convertible bonds. My business has more money than it could ever want now."

"Convertible bonds are the same instrument that stung me. Who purchased the bonds?"

"Mr. Winthrop."

Printed in the United States
By Bookmasters